Borderlands

Alan Cash

First published in 2023 by
The Irregular Special Press
for Baker Street Studios Ltd
Endeavour House
170 Woodland Road, Sawston
Cambridge, CB22 3DX, UK

Overall © Baker Street Studios Ltd, 2023
Text © remains with the author

All rights reserved

No parts of this publication may be reproduced, stored in retrieval systems or transmitted in any form or by any means, electronic, mechanical, photocopying, recording or otherwise, except brief extracts for the purposes of review, without prior permission of the publishers.

Any paperback edition of this book, whether published simultaneously with, or subsequent to, the case bound edition, is sold subject to the condition that it shall not by way of trade, be lent, resold, hired out or otherwise disposed of without the publisher's consent, in any form of binding or cover other than that in which it was published.

This is a work of fiction. Names, characters, businesses, places, events and incidents are either the products of the author's imagination or used in a fictitious manner. Any resemblance to actual persons, living or dead, or actual events is purely coincidental.

ISBN: 978-1-901091-89-2

Cover Concept © Anne Nicholls
Cover Picture © Elizabeth Green

Typeset in 8/11$\frac{1}{2}$/18pt Caslon

This book is dedicated to the village of Borth,
Ceredigion, Mid Wales

BY THE SAME AUTHOR

THE JANUS EFFECT

THE XANDRA FUNCTION

Chapter 1

We are haunted not only by the dead, but by the living.

It was all John's fault.

Alistair Powell was round his house, as he was every Monday, going on about Liz as usual, when suddenly his friend said –

"All right. Leave her. Go. Just go. Tell you what –"

'*You're grinning that grin of yours,*' Alistair thought, '*What are you up to?*'

John went over to his bookshelves and pulled out a road atlas of the British Isles and put it down on the coffee table. 1993 was in bright large yellow letters at the top of the front cover.

"This year's edition just out. Now take this pin between your thumb and forefinger."

"What?"

"Do it."

"Okay."

"Now close your eyes. And don't peek!"

"What?"

"If you say "what" once more ..."

Alistair heard the book open. "Right. Stick a pin in the page. No. Try again. No. Again." John sighed. "Okay. Best of three. Right. Open your eyes."

Alistair squinted down at the map. "Aberceldy?" Never heard of it."

"Well, you have now."

*****

The incoming tide, only fifty yards away, growled as it rolled the pebbles.

'All that raw power,' Alistair thought, *'could easily sweep this long one street village into the Irish Sea in minutes.'*

The wind ruffled his sparse hair as he took another pull at his lager and stared moodily over the grey flecked sea.

The volume of pub conversation all around him on the decking suddenly lowered.

"Mind if I join yer?"

A small, squat man, grey hair flaring from underneath a grimy denim cap, sat down opposite, blocking the view.

"Ent seen you afore."

"No, I'm new here."

The man scratched his nose.

"Word is you've taken on old Evans's house past the lifeboat station up by the cliff."

"Is it now?" Alistair said warily. He was getting a sinking feeling about this man – *'but he certainly gets to the point,'* he thought. He took another pull at his diminishing lager

"Wun't sell f'rages. They had to drop the price loads."

"Really. Where do you live?"

"Sorry. Forgettin' meself. Name's Jeff." He extended a rough hand, flecked with pink paint. Alistair took it gingerly.

"Is there much to do around here?"

The man half smiled, showing uneven nicotined teeth "People don' come 'ere for the –ah-*entertainment.*"

"Well?"

"Free pubs, amusements in an ole garage, line dancin' in the 'all – thass about yer lot."

"I mean in the evenings?"

The man worked his mouth and stared at him for a moment. Then he said, "Mos' people keep in after dark." He leant forward conspiratorially and whispered, "Afraid of 'The Shinies'."

"The what?"

The man tapped the side of his nose and winked.

'That settles it', thought Alistair, *'your genuine copper bottomed nutter'*.

"The Shinies?" he said, politely.

The man nodded, got up, leant towards him, tapped the side of his nose again and then lumbered off across the creaking boards.

Alistair watched him go, but found he was looking straight into the gaze of other drinkers. The moment he caught their eye they looked down again or continued their conversation in low voices.

The man did not come back.

Alistair was relieved, but at the same time disquieted. What if everyone was like that? He felt very much the outsider. The only other person he'd met in this part of the world had been the solicitor in Traethmor eight miles away, who was acting for the deceased's estate. Everything else had been done on the phone. The conveyancing had taken months. But the house had jumped out at him in the estate agent's particulars as being within his very low price bracket. It had a wonderful view so why had the price been so low? It had worried him then. It worried him now. Still, for better or worse, he was here now and here he was going to stay. Too late to change his mind now. The money had gone through and he'd picked up the keys that afternoon from reception. The secretary had been keen to get off. It was Thursday. Perhaps she had something planned. *'Never liked Thursdays'* he thought. Thursday was the day he broke up with Liz.

He looked at his watch. It was getting on for 7:30. The sun was sinking in front of him as an orange ball, soon to disappear below the horizon. It had been a perfect autumn day.

He took a last gulp of his drink and got up to go. Again several people looked his way and then down again. He felt unsettled, but tried to smile, as if to ward them off.

The entrance to the inside of the pub was down a short flight of steps and under a low lintel. As soon as he opened the door the noise and fug enveloped him. He carried his glass to the bar. The barman put down his polishing cloth, smiled, and took it from him.

"Good night, Sir, come again!"

Alistair smiled in return but said nothing. He nodded and made for the low door. He wasn't used to this politeness at home. He must stop thinking like this. This would this was 'home' now.

Out on the long street, a cool salty breeze blew in his face. He pulled up the hood of his anorak. What a stupid time to move house with the winter coming on! But he felt he *had* to get away now, get away from *her*.

His steel heeled shoes rang in the stillness. Streetlights began to flicker on, first red and then warming up to orange. But there were too few of them to hold back the encroaching night. Gloom rolled down from the surrounding hills and particularly from the tall cliff at the end of the village, topped by a war memorial he could see from his house.

As he approached the chip shop the multi-coloured lamps, strung in an inverted 'V' over the apex of its roof, abruptly shut off and, as he went past, the warm yellow light that had been cascading from it onto the pavement disappeared.

It was the same when he reached the gift emporium near the corner shop, a great barn of a place, with an amusement arcade attached. Instant oblivion. Then the lights went out ahead of him in the corner shop, as if in response to a prearranged signal. He was beginning to feel really shut out. All the houses he had passed had closed their curtains against the darkness.

Aberceldy was shut up for the night.

He passed the corner shop on the left, walking quickly down the back road behind the row of houses, their backs turned resolutely away from him, hunched forward, facing the sea. The lane was unlit, save for one small old-fashioned lamp halfway down, almost opposite the rear of his house.

Reaching his back yard he turned right and unfastened the stiff hook that held the green wooden gate closed. It squeaked open in the stillness.

Turning to re-fasten it he glanced up the lane and thought he saw a shadow, or something, shoot across the mouth at its junction with the main road. He went quickly up the steps to the back door.

Keys, keys- they were never where you thought they were. Not in any of the five pockets of his anorak. Eventually he ran them to ground in his right-hand fleece pocket. Stuck at the top of the steps outside the kitchen door he felt strangely conspicuous - naked even – struggling to get in out of the night.

'*This is silly*', he thought, '*who could possibly be watching me?*' The tops of the windows of the caravans on the field behind the hedge across the lane were barely above the level of the foliage.

He let himself in, closed the door and leant against it, momentarily disorientated. This was the first time he'd entered in the dark. Where was the light switch? He knew it was somewhere over by the door into the hall.

He waited for a moment, letting his eyes adjust. In the silence he thought he could just hear the sea breathing in and out. Then he walked tentatively across the creaking floor and put his hand out, feeling for the switch –

Bang!

He ducked instinctively and then turned quickly to see and hear something hit the window, bounce once in the yard, and disappear.

The hooligans! Messing about at this time of night. Thought they'd annoy the newcomer did they? He'd show them!

He wrenched open the door, skidded down the steps, ran across the yard to the wall, ready to shout at the laughing, retreating forms.

Nothing.

Not a soul about.

No suspicious scuffling from the dark hedge across the lane – just the slow breathing of the sea at high tide, gnawing at the pebbles.

The lane glistened, empty.

A train rattled past in the distance, just below the smudge of the hills, its carriage lights flickering between the trees.

He looked up at the kitchen window. There was a greyish white mark on it. He went up the steps and leaned out from them, braced against the balustrade, scratched a fingernail across the imprint and brought the scraping up to his nose. Salty. It had a gritty feel to it.

He went inside and turned on the light, looked closely at the imprint. Memories from his childhood flooded back. Of his father, red-faced, blowing into a football carcass, inflating the leather ball and lacing it up. The pattern on the glass was familiar from the million times he had booted a sandy ball, fresh from a game on the beach, against the yard wall of their rented holiday home. The lacing stood out starkly against the almost perfect round splodge. But who would have such a thing now? They were out of the ark.

He turned back to the room, with its solitary naked bulb swinging slightly from the ceiling. Someone had made a half-hearted attempt to put some yellow emulsion on the tired greying walls, but had made no effort to touch the dark brown paint on the woodwork. The rest of the house was worse – early 20th-century chocolate brown was on the walls everywhere. Even on a sunny day it would give you the creeps – but at this time of night ... he shivered and closed the door into the yard. No wonder it was so cheap.

He went into the hall, turned on the light for the landing upstairs, went into the sitting room and switched on the single ceiling globe. Light! He must have more light. That would be the first thing he would buy when he went into Traethmor.

The shabby brown three-piece suite squatted sullenly on the black and white flecked carpet. The only picture in the room was of a sludgy brown seascape. It was 'enough to give you the pip' as his father would have said.

Beyond the dwarf wall to the narrow front yard the road glistened blackly. Two widely spaced low-power streetlamps stood gaunt against the darkness.

He pulled the curtains across the bay window, the old fashioned rings grating protestingly over the rails, and put on one bar on the ancient electric fire, afraid to blow the wiring. That would be another thing he would have to get. More heat! The list was endless. The whole place needed re-wiring. Perhaps a bit of DIY would lift his spirits over the weekend before he went for an interview for that job as a journalist on the local paper on Monday.

He went back into the kitchen and looked again at the imprint on the window. Who would play football at this time of night?

He turned off the light and closed the door, making his way slowly upstairs. There was nothing else to do tonight.

When he was up there, he realised he'd left the lights on downstairs. He looked over the banisters. A strange feeling of dread came over him. He didn't want to go down there again – it was somehow creepy. Once he was down, he wouldn't want to go up again – the dark at his back. That brown decor had to go – even if he had to take a blowtorch to it! At that thought he felt a cold twinge up his back, as if someone had laid a clammy hand on it. He shook himself. This was daft. Come on, get a grip.

The master bedroom had two beds, one of which he had made up – the one furthest from the window. It was chilled – still hadn't warmed up despite several hot water bottles he had put in to air it. He got into bed almost fully clothed, turned out the light by the long pull cord and tried to go to sleep.

"Good morning," she said, raising her tousled red hair from her pillow. She smiled, showing a gap in her upper teeth. The sun shone through the curtains behind her. Her warmth thrilled through him.

He found it difficult to speak. "Is it?" was all he could manage. *A strange reply*, he thought, absently.

"For me it is, now that I've found you."

He jolted awake. One streetlight could just be seen through the thin curtain. It had seemed so real. It had been morning. This totally unknown but captivating woman had been lying next to him – her warmth so real, her smell so …

He shivered in the damp sheets. He really must set about airing the house properly. He lay there on his back, thinking about her. There was something familiar about her and yet not familiar. That gap-toothed smile …

The sound of an inadequately silenced motorbike woke him again. But this time it really was day. The memory of her was still with him – stronger than ever.

Today was Friday, wasn't it? He glanced at the bedside clock 8.30 already! Where were all those good intentions? He'd have a quick breakfast and go out for a paper.

He came downstairs, forgetting the lights were still on. This was no way to save the planet! He went round switching them off.

When he went into the sitting room he noticed a fragrance, like a woman's perfume. For a moment it was quite strong and then it dissipated as if it had never been. The room was cold and he had the strangest feeling that someone wanted to get at him, but something or someone was holding it back with difficulty. He shook himself trying to get rid of the crawling sensation up his back. He dragged back the curtains. Watery sunshine flooded in.

He went into the hall. Daylight was coming through the half glazed inner front door to his left. He looked through it, just in case there was any post, even at this early stage. A piece of white paper was lying on the concrete in the enclosed porch. There was no writing on it.

He unlocked the door and bent down to pick it up. It came away limply, damp from the moisture coming in under the outer door. He laid it over his left hand and brought it in.

Turning it over he found an invitation – the ink blurred and runny. 'Aberceldy Welcome Group. Meets every Monday, 7.30. Neuadd Goffa. Come along and get to know us.' There was no telephone number. Just turn up, he supposed. He wondered who they might be. Perhaps they knew something about the house and why it was scaring him so much.

Chapter 2

He stood holding the damp letter. Monday was three days away. In the meantime, he must get on with the house. You could be scared anywhere.

He went into the kitchen. Already the football imprint was degrading in the sun. Soon it would be gone.

In the sunshine things seemed less worrying. Perhaps there was a perfectly logical reason for everything. But he couldn't quite shake off the atmosphere in the house. Perhaps Jones had died in the sitting room. He shivered.

Breakfast. Need breakfast. Get the blood sugar up. He looked in the cupboard. Only cereal and a loaf. That would have to do.

The corner shop was sold out of his favourite newspaper, so it meant a longish walk to the newsagent he'd spotted last night.

The village was coming back to life. Two dogs were playing on the piece of waste ground next to the gift emporium.

As he crossed the road the door of the shop opened and a bearded man appeared, heaving out a rusting wheeled rack full of buckets and spades.

Alistair waved at him, "Lovely day!"

"It is that!" The man parked the contraption on the concrete apron and went back inside.

"Brown Girl in the Ring" was exuding loudly from the open door of the amusements.

Blustery wind threw squawking seagulls about as he dodged couples shepherding their progeny along the pavement, already sucking ice lollies.

The paper shop was on a corner of a narrow lane separating it from a shop selling pine furniture.

There was nobody about. It was dim inside because of all the items crowding the windows. Stuff was piled everywhere, even scaling the walls in gravity defying cliffs.

He spotted the rack of newspapers and magazines over on the left and made towards them, just as a small man wearing glasses materialised from the dark doorway behind the counter. He looked worried and a cigarette hung from his thin lips.

"Have you got a Telegraph?"

"Over there, if we've got one."

"Thanks."

As he paid for it and the man worked the ancient till to give him his change, he tried to start a conversation –

"I was talking to a man in the Queen's Head last night and he mentioned someone or something called 'The Shinies'.

The man looked pained. "Oh, yes?"

"Said his name was Jeff."

"Oh. Yes. Jeff. Shouldn't be taking much notice of him. Touched he is like."

"Touched?"

The man made a twirling motion with a finger next to the side of his head.

"So what or who are they?"

"Didn't buy him a drink did you? Always anglin' for a drink he is."

"No. He left before I could offer."

"Well, I wouldn't take any notice if I was you."

"No?"

"No."

"Well, thanks anyway. See you again."

"It's a small village." The man turned and disappeared into his dark hole.

'Charming', he thought as he made his way out. The musty smell in the shop made him gasp as he met the cool fresh air. *'Well, he won't bite will he?'*

He went back in. The man was standing behind the counter, just lighting up another cigarette.

"Where's he live?"

"Who?"

"Jeff."

"Boatyard up the estuary."

"Is it far?"

"Far enough."

"Right."

As he came out the sky darkened and the wind got up. Raindrops started studding the pavement, kicking up windblown sand. He thrust the paper inside his fleece and took shelter underneath the Pine Shop's awning. People rushed past holding a variety of oddments above their heads in a fruitless attempt to ward off the downpour.

As it showed no sign of improving he set off, buffeted by the squall, until he reached the corner shop, when it shut off as abruptly as it had begun.

By the time he reached his back yard the sun had come out. Typical!

Inside he closed the squeaking back door behind him and, casting his damp fleece aside on the kitchen table, went into the front room and flopped down in one of the wing chairs. He sneezed as the dust erupted from it.

He scanned the headlines on the front page and then turned to the Features section as was his custom, folding the paper so he was ready to read the first broadsheet page of it.

And dropped the paper.

The woman from his dream looked up at him.

Underneath her face, which was in black and white, was the headline 'Amelia Earhart: New evidence found'. Her mouth was tightly closed. Perhaps to hide her gap-toothed grin, he thought.

Everybody knew about her mysterious disappearance – at least he did. It turned up in every badly written book on disappearances along with the tired cliches that bulked out every newspaper article – 'Lucky' Lucan, Donald Crowhurst, Glenn Miller, Manchester Football Club –

He got up, and ran out into the kitchen. But the rain had washed the imprint away.

Come on now, get a grip. Just some local lads playing with their father's old football –

He sat back down in the front room. Looked down at her face. He imagined Freud chuckling. A replacement woman, Ja?

He looked round the room. The brown paint was really getting him down. He would start small – obliterate the dark hall out of existence with some bright colour.

He'd take a bracing walk along the beach and then after lunch – Traethmor for a paint shop.

He pulled on his anorak and walking boots, dragged the sticking outer door shut behind him and swiftly crossed the road.

The tide was going out as he slithered and scrunched his way over the stones down to the drying beach.

Rocks, strewn with seaweed, jutted from the base of the cliffs to his left. Small children clambered amongst the rock pools earnestly waving nets of bright orange and green.

He was divided about children. Someone to be proud of (hopefully), but a great drain on one's income (definitely) – keeping you tied to your job – and didn't the boss know it. Better off as he was – freelance, childless, writer and journalist.

He turned right and set off at a good pace, leaving uneven footprints as his weak right ankle leaned heavily to one side.

He passed the ends of wooden breakwaters that marched out fifty yards or so from the shingle. Gulls shrieked overhead.

Somewhere would be the drowned forest mentioned in all the guidebooks. Out there in the bay was the mythical country Cantraer Y Gwaelod, inundated one night when the drunkard master of the sluices failed to close them against the incoming tide. On calm summer evenings it was said you could hear the bells of the city tolling in dismay under the waves.

Up ahead he saw two dark parallel lines at 45° to the beach disappearing into the sea. They were like Neolithic tramlines. Coming up to one he kicked it experimentally. It had a rubbery texture.

"I'd be glad if you didn't do that," a cultured male voice said behind him.

Alistair turned round, startled out of his thoughts. Hurrying towards him was a middle-aged man of middle height, sporting a huge brown beard. His hands were stuffed into an all-enveloping duffle coat. Watery blue eyes peered at him.

"And you are?" asked Alistair.

"Archie Dugdale, amateur archaeologist."

"Dugdale?" Alistair suppressed a laugh.

"I know. I've heard them all."

"And this is the drowned forest, I presume?"

Archie removed his hands from his pockets and rubbed them together. "Yes. A bit of it, anyway. Remarkably fine specimen, don't you think?" The wind blew his hair in his eyes and he paused to brush it away distractedly. "Come over here and look. See? With a bit of imagination it could be a man-made causeway, perhaps a ceremonial way through the forest, out along the foreshore leading to the Henge."

"The Henge?"

"You've heard of Sea Henge of course – the one on the East Anglian coast?"

"Vaguely."

This is only a little one, of course. It's out there – you can just see a bit of it sticking up above the water. At low tide you can see a lot more. They've had divers out and everything. 'Course it's not here all the time – the beach shifts. But we've been very lucky this year."

"You mean this was a place of ritual?"

"Oh, yes. Very much so. Can you imagine them hauling their local prince or shaman along here on a burial sledge, placing him in the middle of the Henge and waiting for the waters to float it off, bearing it away to the realm of the gods?"

"That would depend on the sea level."

"I know, I know. But I can dream, can't I? They do say this place is still used for ritual – I've seen lights from my house on Midsummer nights."

"Where do you live then?"

He swung round and pointed. "Just over there – that pink cottage, behind the barrier. And you?"

"Past the lifeboat station, along the front. I've just moved in."

"Then you must drop by sometime. We always like to make newcomers feel welcome you know, in the village."

"That's very nice of you. What's your place called?"

"Tintagel."

"Naturally! Good luck with the digging!"

Archie looked pained. "Oh, shan't be doing any of that. Just taking some core samples."

"And there you were telling me not to kick it!"

"Ah, but I'm more scientific."

"Right. I'm Alistair Powell by the way." He held out his hand and Archie wrung it warmly.

"Pleased to meet you. In most evenings. Just knock."

Alistair smiled, waved and turned away.

When he got as far as the dilapidated Grand Hotel and the 1960s concrete sea wall he called it a day. Walking back along the beach the wind got up – the famous 'Celdy Wind'.

The Henge mound was now more apparent. Archie was no longer around otherwise he would have asked him more about the twisted trunks that had surfaced in the sand, some with pools ground out beneath them by the tide. If you squatted beside them they became mysterious forests, mountain ranges covered in lush vegetation instead of rubbery logs coated in seaweed.

He exchanged brief greetings with a number of hardy fishermen that had set their rods up pointing out to sea, studying the undulating grey surface.

When he got back, he felt chilled and brewed himself some tea.

He was just settling down with the papers when a series of sharp knocks on the back door brought him back to his feet.

In the kitchen, outlined against the frosted glass of the half-glazed door was the shadow of a shortish figure. He glanced out of the window sideways to see a woman with red brown hair standing patiently on the top step. Thirties, possibly.

He opened the door. "Yes?"

"Mr Powell?"

"Yes."

She stuck out a chubby hand. "I'm Angharad, your next-door neighbour – other half of this semi."

"Come in, come in."

"Thanks. Have you got a minute?"

"Sure. Just made some tea – would you …?"

"Thanks."

He got another mug from the cupboard by the cooker.

"Milk and sugar?"
"Just milk."
"Haven't any biscuits. Just moved in."
"I know."
"Come on through."
She perched awkwardly on the settee, her dark tartan skirt barely covering her chunky knees.
"Saw you come in from the beach. Sorry to impose. Just wanted to mention about my brother."
"Your brother?"
"I was in the back, see, at the newsagents. Heard you in the shop."
"Ah."
"People think he's touched."
"Go on."
"He's not really. Since my sister-in-law died, he's never been the same. Devoted they were."
"Ah. I see. He was married to her?"
"I'm afraid they're a pet subject of his."
"What are?"
"Ghosts. Souls of people who went missing before their time. Trying to find their way back to the land of the living."
'Same directness', he thought, 'doesn't mess about'. "Has anyone else seen them?"
"The Greys."
"And who are they?"
"Very odd. Meet in the deconsecrated chapel down by the railway line."
"Well, I assure you – er –"
"Angharad."
"That I'm not in the habit of rushing to judgement about people."
She smiled. "I was sure you'd understand."

"Yes?"

"I can see it in your face."

There was an awkward silence.

"Jeff said no one would touch this house."

She clasped her knees and looked down. "That's right ..."

"Shall I put the fire on? It is a bit chilly isn't it?"

She looked up and smiled. Those brown eyes were really quite appealing.

"It always is. Mr Jones would never spend a penny on it. 'Till his dying day ... Oh don't worry, he didn't die in here."

"That's a relief."

"No. In hospital in Traethmor."

"Thank goodness for that."

"I could see it was worrying you. Look I must go – shouldn't be holding you up."

"That's all right. I wonder if you could help me? This brown paint – do you know where there's a good paint shop?"

"I can draw you a map."

"Oh, thanks very much. I'll get some paper and a pen."

"Now as you come down the hill into Traethmor, see, turn left at the bottom and it's just here – Kendricks."

"Thanks. That's most helpful."

"I must go. Perhaps I'll see you again?"

"I hope so too."

He watched her trip down the steps. Quite pretty in a dumpy sort of way – so unlike angular tall Liz. You could imagine ... Stop it, Alistair.

Right. To business. He got out the car and even caught himself whistling. Why not? The air was fresh, the sun was out. He had left his old life behind. And yet something unpleasant hovered at the edges of his conscious mind.

Soon he was on the open road, windows down, radio on, eating up the eight or so miles to Traethmor.

Around this time of the afternoon there were often little gems on Radio 4 – fifteen minute programmes. Surfacing from the subdued murmur the announcer's voice suddenly came over unnaturally loud, "Alternate reality. Doors between worlds? Arthur Parry discusses parallel universes with Professor Barry Grenfell PhD, FRS."

One of the things that came up was the Vaughan family near Gloucester in 1905. Three children – boy aged ten and two sisters, five and three, had been playing in a field, but failed to return for lunch. Despite an extensive search no trace of them was found until four days later when a farm labourer found them fast asleep in a ditch, metres from the house.

* * * * *

He came over the crest of a hill. Below him the town was the spread out against a sparkling sea punctuated by spires and the broken tower of an ancient castle.

He found a parking spot and followed Angharad's map. Up a quiet side street was a small shop packed tight with DIY stuff. People were chatting unintelligibly in Welsh. It really was a foreign country.

He approached a rather dour looking woman behind the counter.

"I was thinking of repainting the kitchen – maybe in yellow. And the hall is a disgusting chocolate brown and –

"Idris!" she called into the back of the shop, "One for you y'ere!"

"Just moved in have you?"

"Er yes …"

Idris emerged from the back of the shop – short cropped grey hair and a pencil behind one ear.

"I was looking for some advice …"

"How big is the kitchen, then?"

"Oh, about ten feet by twelve."

"Shouldn't have something too overpowering then. What sort of colour is it going over?"

"Nasty sort of gone-off white."

"Ah. Need a good wash down with sugar soap and an undercoat now …"

After about twenty minutes, loaded down with paint, scrapers, brushes and the like he began to think he'd taken on too much. The bill was horrifying.

"Do you know a good decorator?"

Idris picked up a card from the counter. "Local man. Not far from y'ere. If you go now you might just catch him. I'll just help you with this stuff to the car."

"Oh, thanks very much."

Having loaded up he looked at his watch. Might still be time.

"Just down there, sir. First left, second right."

"Thanks."

Ah well. S'pose it'll do no harm to get a quote.

He spotted number 28 almost immediately. A terraced house in a narrow road, cars parked on either side on the pavements giving only a very narrow space for pedestrians to squeeze past. He rang the bell.

A dog started barking immediately. He had half a mind to walk away. Didn't like dogs – and they knew it. Perhaps they could see something he couldn't. The scratching at the door and snuffling under the gap at the bottom unnerved him.

Then he heard a very Welsh voice calling the dog off and the door opened on a tall, stooped man with a wispy moustache and balding head, hanging onto the collar of a large black dog that was constantly trying to leap forward.

"Can I help you?" It was a pleasant, open face.

"I was looking for Mr Jones." The dog started on a series of deep growls and barks, barely drawing breath and trying to get at him. "I got this card from Kendricks," he said, holding it up.

"Quiet, Pluto! That's me. What can I do for you?"
"Just moved into the area –"
"Quiet, I say!"
"Aberceldy – on the front, just near the lifeboat …"
"Gwen! Come and deal with this dog will you?"
Someone came into the dark hall and hauled the dog away.
Jones looked relieved. "That's better. Sorry about all that. Aberceldy, you say? Name of the house?"
"Glaswern".
The man's face suddenly clouded. "That house doesn't want to be painted. Sorry. Can't help you. Good day." And the door closed.
"Right." Alistair was left on the pavement holding the card.
'That house doesn't want to be painted', not 'that house needs painting'. He shivered in the cold street, the sun no longer shining over the houses.
He remembered the wall in the kitchen – it looked as if someone had started and then abruptly stopped.
It was true that the house was a time capsule – hadn't been touched for years – but to attribute feelings to a house … But hadn't he been doing just that?
He hoped not every painter in the area felt that way. He couldn't face doing the job on his own.

Chapter 3

It was somehow quicker coming back. He squeezed the car into the garage and carried his purchases across the yard, up the back steps and into the kitchen, clumping them down on the enamelled table top.

Then it struck him how hungry he was. He had meant to stock up in Traethmor, but that visit to the painter had unnerved him. *'That house doesn't want to be painted.'*

He looked nervously at the wall. The jagged slash of yellow against the greying white looked sickly, jaundiced.

But the sun was shining, the birds were singing, a tractor could be heard in the distance – and then the sound of a rattling train going past.

What was he worrying about? He looked at the window. Perfectly clean – as if nothing had ever happened.

It meant another trip to the corner shop. By the time he had put the steak pie in the oven, peeled an assortment of vegetables and put them on to cook it was beginning to get dusk, even though it was only 5.30.

When it was ready he moved the painting stuff off the kitchen table and sat down to eat. The sounds of the day were becoming muted, if not entirely silent, except for the murmuration of starlings, swinging about the sky in their intricate patterns, settling and taking off again endlessly until they finally disappeared.

The long evening stretched in front of him. The silence that he thought he had craved became gradually more and more oppressive.

He went into the sitting room, but didn't draw the curtains, hanging onto the last of the daylight, watching the sun set over the sea until it disappeared into a bank of cloud low on the horizon.

He turned on the light, sat down and turned on the radio, tuning into Radio Three, as the voices on Radio Four would distract him from reading – but he needed some kind of background noise.

He picked up the paper, deciding to avoid reading any more about Amelia Earhart. She was beginning to get to him. Best forget all about her. Bury himself in the business section. That was it.

He woke up with a jolt.

Someone was in the room. He could feel it. He looked round. Nothing. The feeling dissipated instantly. The radio was still warbling on- some totally unidentifiable symphony.

The feeling may have gone, but the room was freezing. It had crept up his legs into his knees. He lurched to his feet and put on the ancient three bar fire. He didn't dare put on all three bars in case it blew the wiring. The survey had said the house would need a complete rewire.

He needed to hear a human voice – not just one on Radio Four. He would ring John. It was his fault he was here anyway.

He took his mobile out of his pocket. No signal. Perhaps it would be better in the kitchen – he'd seen a mast on the skyline at the back.

He crossed the dark hall and clicked down the switch in the kitchen.

Instantly saw a reflection of himself in the window opposite – white and haggard with stubble. He looked like a dropout – worse, as if he'd been sleeping rough under a hedge for a week.

Here the signal was stronger, but not brilliant. He paused. What would he say? *"John, I've had this strange experience. I thought there was someone in the room with me."* Oh, come on! What sort of idiot would he take him for?

Maybe he could go next door? Angharad seemed a friendly sort. At least she would be company. Yeah, just land yourself on her why don't you, when you've hardly met – in the state you look?

He made himself a cup of tea and went back into the sitting room. He'd never been a believer in ghosts or spirits of any kind. And he wasn't going to start now. Just one of those strange things that happen in the interval when you're just going off to sleep or waking up. That's all.

He tuned the radio to Radio Four. "Alternate reality. Doors between worlds?" The sonorous announcer intoned. What was he in? Some kind of time warp? It had been an entrancing programme out in the open country, with the sun gleaming on the trees – but now it felt altogether different, threatening. He shut it off.

Of course, he thought, looking at his watch, it's 9.30 – only a repeat. That's when they put the repeats on.

But only for a half-hour programme. The programme had been fifteen minutes long.

He sat back in the chair. Felt hemmed in. He switched on the radio again, rapidly retuning to Radio Three. It started okay, but then became distorted.

He couldn't stay in the room anymore. Perhaps it was just this room. Other rooms might be okay. Perhaps Jones really did die in this room and Angharad, seeing the worry cross his face, had abruptly switched to say he had died in hospital.

He got up and bent down to switch off the fire.

"Don't do that!"

A distorted thunderclap of voices in his head, both male and female, some old, some young.

He whipped round, falling full-length on the carpet.

"Now look what you've done!" It was *the* voice. The voice of the woman in his dream.

"We're sorry. But we're so cold!" The susurration of voices clamoured in his head.

The voice of the woman was warm, but commanding. "Be quiet everyone. We must take care of him. He's the first one for years. The first Lamplighter we've had for so long."

He put his hands over his ears. "Go away! Leave me alone!"

He felt rather than heard a murmur of assent and the voices faded away.

"You see, they're drawn like moths to a flame. You have the aura."

He raised his head from the floor.

"Where are you?"

"Inside your head."

"I'm not imagining you?"

"No. I'm going now. The shock has been too great, but they are almost uncontrollable."

"Who are they?"

Silence

"Who are they?"

No answer.

He stumbled out of the room and into the kitchen, dragging the mobile phone from his pocket.

"John, John is that you?"

"Hello? Who's that?"

"It's Alistair, Alistair!"

"You sound terrible. I'll just turn the sound down." There was a roar of canned laughter, suddenly muted. "Right. That's better. What's the matter?"

"They talked to me, said I was a Lamplighter."
"You're talking gibberish man! Get a grip!"
Alistair tried to calm his feverish breathing.
"She was inside my head."
"Who was?"
"Amelia bloody Earhart!"
"What?"
"Amelia Earhart. She spoke to me."
"And you know what this Earhart woman sounds like do you?"
"I don't know, I don't know!"
"So how do you know it was her?"
"It's too complicated to explain."
"All right. So say it was her. Where did she speak to you?"
"In the front room of my house."
"In Aberceldy?"
"In Aberceldy."
"And had you just woken up?"
"Not long."
"Ah."
"What do you mean, 'Ah'?"
"And how can I help?"
"I don't know. I just wanted someone to talk to, to tell me I'm not going mad."
"You're not going mad. How long have you been in this house?"
"This is my second night."
"Ah."
"Stop this 'Ah' business will you!"
"Look, there's nothing I can do at this distance – but there is someone who can."
"Who for heaven's sake?"
"Sue."
"What, Sue Masters?"
"The very same."

"And how is she … ?"

The voice chuckled. "I think she's going to pay you a visit. She'll sort you out. Goodbye now."

"But …"

The phone went dead.

Sue … Sue Masters. Coming here? Whatever for?

Sue Masters. Stolid, unimaginative Sue. *Good grief.* What was she doing coming here?

He stood, staring at the wall. Then, very slowly put the mobile in his pocket. He couldn't go back in that room. Somehow in here it felt safer.

Maybe one half of the house …

If that was so, then the bedroom over the top of the sitting room would be just as bad.

He would just have to leave the fire on in the sitting room all night. And the light. Never mind the bills. He just wasn't going back in there until the morning, in the daylight.

He went out into the hall, turned on the light and the light on the landing above and crept up the stairs, pausing to look behind him every now and then. Was something following him? No. He must stop frightening himself.

The bed in the tiny back bedroom at the top of the stairs on the right was not made up and had lots of his junk on it. He turfed it off, took some blankets out of the wardrobe facing the bed and lay down, pulled them over his head and waited for morning.

Chapter 4

"So, do you feel any different about Alistair now he's gone?" Sue said, sitting down at Liz's small kitchen table in her first floor flat.

"I'm still …" Liz pursed her thin lips, "ambivalent."

"Well, you're not getting any younger. How many more are you going to let slip through your fingers?"

"I'm not like you, Sue. I've no desire for children. And that's all men are good for, aren't they? Sex and children. Rest of the time they just bung up the place getting in the way."

"So, you're not looking for companionship – resigned to solo holidays, meals for one … Nobody to share your memories with?" She looked at Liz half mockingly over the rim of her mug of coffee. Despite all the years Liz had known her she still made it too strong for her. She took an experimental sip. '*I wouldn't mind him,*' she thought. '*He isn't all that bad*'.

"Companionship's all right. Just don't want to live with them. They're OK as long as you live separately."

"So you can pick them up and put them down when you feel like it?"

"Yup. That's about it."

Sue decided to probe a little deeper, not something she usually did. "So what's wrong with him? You had been going out for some time. You even moved in with him for a bit."

"He was … fussy and controlling."

"In what way?"

"Wouldn't let me into the kitchen. Always wanted to do things his way. Couldn't bear me to go rooting in the pantry, 'upsetting things', she imitated Alistair's voice.

"A man who cooks. What a find! And you let him get away!" She tutted mockingly.

"It's all very well for you to talk. Your love life isn't exactly brilliant."

"Ah, but I know what's wrong with me. I'm not giving enough and I test relationships to destruction."

"Give and others'll take," Liz said harshly.

Sue stared out of the window at the neat garden with its well kept lawn. Not a dead leaf to be seen, even though it was autumn. The flowers all deadheaded and tied back. And Liz was calling Alistair a control freak! Not like her own garden. An untamed wilderness, and, at the end of the garden, things she couldn't even remember, let alone visit. A gently rotting shed with creepers so thickly entwined over the door that it would be hopeless to get in.

"So you're not going to look for him then," Sue said.

Liz looked into the air above Sue's head. "Don't even know where he is," she said in a bored voice.

"Not even the slightest idea?"

Liz pursed her lips. "Somewhere in Wales I think John said."

Sue made a mental note of that. Maybe Alistair's best friend, also her boss, would know.

"Look, why are you so interested?" Liz asked, getting up, turning to the sink and gazing out over the garden.

"I thought, maybe, you'd want to know- whether he's all right."

"Haven't given it a thought." She sniffed and turned round to Sue, giving her a wintry smile. "If you want him, you can have him- and good riddance!"

"Don't be like that."

"I never want to see him again," Liz said vehemently, sitting down at the table and burying her face in her arms crossed on its surface.

"*God, you're raw,*" Sue thought. Better not say anything else. She'd bought her a present, but now didn't seem like the appropriate moment. Perhaps she'd leave it on the kitchen unit when she went, with the little note attached. Liz could find it later. "Can I get you another coffee?"

"No," came the muffled reply.

"Whatever it was he did, it can't have been that bad. He wasn't seeing another woman was he?"

Again the muffled response. "No."

Sue knew she shouldn't ask, but she couldn't stop herself. "So what was it then?"

Liz raised a red face from her arms. "He photographed me while I was asleep."

"Oh." It didn't seem that bad to Sue. Rather sweet, in fact. Funny how having their picture taken did that to people. Not that she liked having hers done. A bit pear shaped. All right – a lot pear shaped. Freckles hidden by make up, grey eyes hidden by rectangular specs and shortish curly black hair, going grey at the parting. No, on second thought, maybe she wouldn't like to be photographed unawares without her defences on … but then if someone really loved you and wanted a memento of you to look at when away from you … "How did you know?"

"I sort of sensed he'd done something – and then later when I looked through his mobile phone …"

Sue said nothing. She didn't think doing that was very nice, like she was married to him or something and was checking up on him.

Rather an invasion of privacy. Again she saw another side to her friend – one she didn't like. Maybe time for a swift exit. She looked up at the kitchen clock. "Sorry, just noticed the time. Got to rush. Hair appointment."

Liz looked up at her glumly. Her look seemed to say, 'What a total waste of time that'll be.' "Sorry to be such a pain, Sue. I'll give you a ring, OK?"

"Fine. Don't worry. You'll meet someone yet."

"I'm off men for life."

"We all say that."

"I'll get your coat," Liz said, getting up and going out into the hall.

As soon as she had, Sue dug in her shoulder bag and put the small present on the sink drainer and left the room, closing the door.

In the hall Liz gave her perfunctory hug, not like usual. "I'll give you a ring," she said in an oddly hushed tone. Sue wondered whether she would.

As she clomped down the stairs in her high heeled boots, which gave her much needed height, she mulled over what Liz had said. "If you want him, you can have him."

Out in the cool Autumn air tinged with watery sunshine she poked around in her bag for the keys to her second hand silver Peugeot 106 and came to a decision. All right. She would.

No time like the present. Seated in the car amongst the drifts of discarded sweet papers, she pulled out her mobile and rang her boss.

A tired, rather bored voice answered, "John Hunter."

"Not got you out of bed have I?"

"Oh, hi Sue! You all right?" The voice instantly brightened.

"Hope I'm not disturbing you."

"Yes, you are, thank God."

Sue's brow creased. "Where are you?"

"In the office. "

"On a Saturday?"

"Yup. You know I'm in court on Monday. Loads of preparation to do."

Sue knew. Mathews Construction was a tiresome client, but brought in much needed fees to the practice. She had the luxury of being able to close the door on a Friday and forget about it until Monday. John couldn't.

"I won't keep you. D'you know where Alistair's gone?"

The voice on the other end chuckled. "What are you up to?"

"I think Liz secretly misses him. Wouldn't it be nice if we at least put them in touch again and let nature take its course?"

"You scheming minx!"

"Don't let on I phoned you."

"There was a grunt of acceptance. "Er, Aberceldy, I think it was."

"Where on earth is that?"

"Mid Wales, somewhere. On the coast."

"Thanks. See you."

"Bright and early Monday morning. We've got lots to do. None of your excuses!"

Of course the hair appointment was a lie. But she needed time to think. Was she really going to go down to Wales? It would be dark by the time she got there.

Coffee. Need coffee. Something strong and hot. There was a shop nearby. She got out of the car and walked briskly down the street and round the corner.

Zeffirelli's wasn't too full. She bought a cappuccino and sat down at a small table for two. Spilled coffee mingled with a half eaten bun. Plastic stirrers and wet sugar completed the mess – she barely had room to put hers down.

She took a sip of the scalding liquid. Was she really going on a wild goose chase? She stared down at the puddled coffee. The noise of the cafe faded to silence –
The face of Alistair appeared in the liquid. He looked awful. Then she saw him spread full-length on the carpet. She gasped. Oh God! It's happening again. He's in trouble. I know he is. I've got to go …
She got up and ran out into the street. By the time she got to her car she was out of breath and her feet ached. Stupid boots! Who cares how tall you are! Be yourself, you idiot.
She wrenched open the car door and flopped into the driving seat.
She hated these episodes. Were they real or just her overactive imagination? No, this was real – just like 7/7. She had dreamt it happening. And there were other times. She never dared tell anyone except Liz and the look on her face had been enough.
Driving back to her flat she flung a few things in a suitcase, changed into her trainers, looked up Aberceldy – thankfully it was on a railway line – there was no way she was driving all the way there – and train times – on Oracle on her TV and rang for a taxi to Snow Hill station. It being a Saturday there were an adequate number of trains. But she would be catching the last one.
She arrived in Colmore Row with not much time to spare. Crossing the road without looking, barely aware of a horn blasting at her, she ran across the pavement, over the bridge, banging into passengers coming the other way – and arrived breathless at the ticket office.
"Single to Aberceldy, please."
Having paid she suddenly realised she had no idea of the time.
"What time is the next train?".
"4.30. You'll just make it if you run."
"Thanks!"

She ran towards the ticket barrier and then saw something beyond it that brought her up short.

Escalators.

They scared her rigid.

She once got her foot stuck in one in a department store when she was a child – brought the whole place to a standstill. Oh, the cringing embarrassment!

"Can I help you, madam?"

An Indian man in uniform stepped forward as she dithered. "Is there a lift?"

"Just over there to your left."

"Is the 4.30 to Aberceldy on time?"

"That'll be the 5 o'clock train to Traethmor – Yes, madam. It's in the station now."

"Thanks."

She found the lift, pressed the button. Come on! Come on! It descended with much clanking and the doors stuttered open. Her sweaty hand grasped the handle of her case and she ran.

She heard a whistle and just got into the carriage in time, practically falling into the vestibule.

Luckily the train was not packed and she found a seat with a table with only one occupant. The train lurched and she almost fell into the lap of the young man by the window.

"Terribly sorry."

He looked up momentarily from his Thinkpad laptop, grinned and looked away.

She sat down and tried to calm her breathing. Well, she'd done it now.

She was on her way.

Chapter 5

The train rattled on towards the night.

Sue looked out into the darkening landscape.

She was too hot.

Somehow she squeezed out of her coat without jabbing her elbow into the man.

Still too hot.

The black turtleneck jumper would have to go. As she struggled out of it revealing her white blouse, did he sneak a glance of some kind? She felt even hotter.

Then she remembered leaving her bottle of water by the sink. Oh, how she would love a drink! Her glasses had steamed up. She took them off to polish them and instantly the world became softer, more amenable somehow. Perhaps she'd leave them off.

"Where are you going to?"

It was a Welsh voice – coming from the young man.

"Wales."

"Yerss. Where exactly?"

"Are you trying to chat me up?"

"It's a long journey," he said with a smile.

"Aberceldy."

"Me too. Got lodgings for the University there."

"What's it like?"

"Cold, windy, nothing to do."

"Oh." *'What was Alistair doing there?'* she thought. "Only go there to sleep though."

"And study, I hope?"

"You my conscience or something?"

"Sorry, I …"

"Yeah, some of that. Don't go out. Can be creepy in the evenings."

Now he's trying to scare me. "So?"

"Long dark main street, not terribly well lit. Mist sweeps in from the sea, fog off the marsh."

"I don't think you're going to get a job with the tourist board any time soon!"

"So what brings you to this hole?"

"Just looking up a friend."

"I'm in the Victorian terrace just outside the station – where's he?"

'I'm not going to tell him I've no idea. What do I do? Think girl!'

"He's coming to pick me up."

The welcome arrival of the drinks trolley cut him short. She put her glasses back on so that she could see what was on it properly. She bought a bottle of water and a chicken sandwich – both ludicrously overpriced. Then the train drew into a station and that brought any further conversation to an end as passengers shuffled past in both directions. What a relief!

She got out her new biography of Shakespeare, turned to the place marked by the post-it note and was immediately transfixed.

It seemed no time had passed at all, but when she looked up for a moment she caught sight of herself in the window. It was now black out there. Staring back at her was a round face with a blob of a nose and short, slightly curly black hair going grey at the parting.

She must get that seen to. Don't want to be thought of as "the badger."

The carriage lights suddenly dimmed – and then went out altogether. There was a collective intake of breath from the passengers and then there were anxious cries.

For some strange reason Sue looked out of the window.

Alistair's face was out there in the darkness, his hands over his ears. He was shouting.

Oh no, it's happening again …

She closed her eyes.

The lights flickered back on.

"Are you all right? You've gone quite pale," a voice said.

She opened her eyes. Alistair was gone.

She turned. The young man looked genuinely concerned. She wiped her forehead with a hand. "I'm okay. Just thought I saw something – that's all."

"Funny about those lights, though."

'Yes. It was. Was it me?' she thought, frightened all over again.

"Never mind. We'll be there soon. Nearly ten past seven," the youth said.

She gasped. Where had all the time gone?

Already she could feel the train slowing and looked out to see its lights reflected off the odd building flashing by.

The speakers came to life. "Aberceldy! Aberceldy station. Please make sure you have all your belongings with you. Cambrian Rail hopes you had a pleasant trip and will travel with us again."

Only a few people were getting off. The rest, she supposed were going on to Traethmor.

She dragged her case off the rack and got out into the night. A stiff breeze was blowing carrying the sound of sheep bleating.

With a swish, squeak and grind the tube of lights rattled off into the darkness.

"Maybe I'll see you around."

The voice of the student made her jump.

"Yes, maybe," she said vaguely, watching him disappear through the dark hole of the exit.

She stood alone on the platform. What on earth was she going to do now? She ventured through the doorway, crossed a small room and stood at the top of a ramp leading down into a dimly lit road. In the distance a car went past left to right, tyres swishing.

Conscious of the wheels of her case grumbling down the concrete and reverberating off the houses on either side, she came down the ramp and stopped again.

The terraced houses, their curtains uniformly drawn, seemed to funnel all passengers forward.

As she rumbled forward the sound of the sea became louder until she reached the left hand corner where the salt wind hit her like a wall.

She shivered in her coat. Even with everything on again it sliced through her.

She turned to her right. The road disappeared into darkness. There seemed to be nothing that way. Forcing herself against the wind she staggered along the pavement to her left.

There were no houses yet on her right, just the sea hissing and scrabbling at the pebbles. On her left tall terraced houses interspersed with tiny cottages shielded her from the darkness.

A squall of rain came sweeping in from the sea and she stopped to wipe her glasses. In the momentary calm she heard something creaking above her.

She looked up. Swinging from rusty chains, lit by a wan light was a sign 'The Artemis Guesthouse'. The curtains were drawn in the double fronted house and the front door had a low board across it. In the window next to her, backed by a curtain, was a notice 'Entrance round the side. Vacancies.'

Well, that was a relief.

She rounded the corner, partially out of the wind. There were steps up to a recessed door with a bell push beside it. She pressed it and a feeble buzz sounded.

Nothing happened.

She kept pressing in a frenzy of feeble buzzing. She was about to knock on the glass when she heard the sound of canned laughter and light appeared in the dark hall. The door creaked open.

A fat unshaven jowly man in a sleeveless cardigan and grey ill-fitting trousers stood looking down at her. Fetid air redolent of boiled cabbage and cats wafted out.

"Good evening," she said. "Sorry to bother you. Have you got a room for the night?"

The man removed the damp dog end from his mouth and coughed.

"Booked have you?"

"No – I ..."

"We're closed for the season, see." The voice was deep, growling and very Welsh. The door began to close.

"It says vacancies in the window. Look I'm cold and wet and the last train's gone and ..."

The man turned "Rhiannon!"

No reply

"Rhiannon! There's a girl y'ere wants a room."

The canned laughter came again, "What is it?"

"I said there's a ..."

"All right, all right." A very fat short little woman in a pinny with crinkly white hair Kirby gripped to her head came up the corridor leaning heavily on a stick.

"Duw, cariad, you look frozen stiff. Come in, come in, yes, yes, yes."

Sue dragged her case in and closed the door gratefully, blocking out the night.

"Where you come from then?"

"Birmingham."

"Goodness! Why didn't you ring?"

'*I don't want to go into long explanations – anyway they would sound totally mad – what to say?*'

"Battery's flat on my mobile and I couldn't get a signal anyway."

"We're in a bit of a fun-ny area round y'ere. You're right. But we're really closed for the season. Forgot to take the sign down in the window. How long you staying then?"

"Oh, about a night –" she saw a frown fit across the woman's face – "Two nights? Would that be okay? I'm supposed to be meeting a friend, but couldn't get through."

The woman's mouth creased. Then she smiled. "Couldn't turn you away on a night like this could I? Just sign the book while I get a key. You just go on up on those young legs of yours. First floor. I'll follow you up."

She looked up the stairs.

Like the north face of Everest.

Right. Shoulder to the wheel. She grasped the banister rail and her suitcase and dragged it, protestingly, up the worn carpet, step by worn carpet step.

The smell of boiled cabbage followed her up.

She arrived at the top, feeling hot again. Below the old lady wheezed up towards her, stick banging on the thin carpet at every step.

"Me arthurritis is giving me what for today, cariad. 'Sno fun gettin' old. On your right. Sea view. Number nine."

Sue inserted the key in the brown door and the lock ground open. The room was high ceilinged, painted in grubby cream and thick brown. There were two single beds, an ancient TV and a wardrobe.

"Bathroom's across the corridor," wheezed the old lady." We're not doing meals this late in the season, but there's a caff down the road. Sleep well, cariad. Here's a front door key. Don't be late in. He bolts the door at 10."

Sue went to the window and looked out.

"Thanks for opening up for me."

"Oh, that's all right. See you in the morning." She closed the door.

Sue turned back gazing into the dark. She could just see the crests of the waves across the road. The sash window rattled in its frame. Dragging the thin curtain over it she sat down on the bed. It sagged.

Where was Alistair? Was he all right? She couldn't wait to get out in the morning and find out.

Chapter 6

Sue sat on the edge of the bed.

No – she couldn't go to bed now.

Her mind was in a whirl. Too much to do. She looked at her watch. Just coming up to 8 o'clock. Time for action! Well, time for something to eat anyway. All she'd had since breakfast was an overpriced chicken sandwich.

She locked her room and crept downstairs. The TV was going full blast so they wouldn't hear. She heaved open the front door and shivered as the cold night air hit her full in the face.

There was a cafe nearby Mrs What's'ername had said. She couldn't bear pubs – the crowds, the smells, the requirement to buy alcohol – and worst of all being a woman on her own.

Alistair loved take-away food, so he might have been somewhere for fish and chips. She might pick up some information at a chippy.

It was easier walking along the street unencumbered by a suitcase. She looked up at the sky. Hurrying clouds periodically gave way to a full moon gazing wanly down.

The pavement was sometimes broad, sometimes narrow, but mostly sloped inwards towards the motley collection of Victorian style villas and converted fishermen's cottages. Their curtains were drawn or, if not, were dark and hollow eyed.

Up ahead on her side, coloured light bulbs flashed an inverted V up the apex of a roof. On getting closer she could see there was a chippy with a narrow over-lit room next to it.

The door to the chip shop stood open. Heat and the smell of hot fat drifted out into the cold.

She joined the queue in front of a huge steel counter. Over the heads of the hard-working staff were coloured panels as to what was on offer with cardboard amendments stuck on with ageing Sellotape.

Eventually her turn came and a middle-aged lady raised an eyebrow to her. She was big bosomed and matronly. Reddened forearms stuck out of a short sleeved nylon overall.

"Is the restaurant open?"

"'Fraid not, love."

"I know, too late in the season."

The woman smiled in recognition. "You been up the Dyson's then?"

"Oh, is that what they're called? At the Artemis?"

"That's them. I don't think they'd appreciate the smell of fish and chips in your room."

"Might ameliorate the smell of boiled cabbage!"

"Hah! I like you! What do you fancy?"

"Cod and chips?"

"Sure. You can eat it next door. Salt and vinegar?"

"No thanks."

Sue paid and the woman smiled again, nodding her head towards the door on the left. "Just through there."

Sue headed through the half glazed door marked 'Staff Only'.

Inside were orange Formica tables just for two people – one either side of the long thin room. The strip lights glared off the white walls. It was really too bright for her, but she'd just have to get used to it. She sat down with her back to the street.

The fish was a bit oily and left a deposit on the roof of her mouth, but the chips were good.

She had just finished and was wondering where to put the wrapping paper when she heard the street door open behind her. A squat man with grey hair flaring out from beneath a dirty blue denim cap, wearing a paint flecked overall, brushed past and sat at a table on the other side of the narrow room facing towards her.

"Don't I know you?" he said.

'*I don't believe it!*' Sue thought. '*I must look desperate.*'

"Don't think so."

He grunted and looked down, but still didn't unwrap his food. "You're with that bloke, aren't you?"

"What bloke?"

"Met him in the pub. Brown hair going a bit thin, beaky nose, about five six."

She stared at him.

"Silver friendship ring on the little finger of his left hand."

Her heart fluttered. She had given him that ring.

"Ah, you do know him then."

The 'Staff Only' door opened and the woman who had served her put her head in.

"You annoying this lady, Jeff?"

"Would I ever?"

"I've got my eye on you. All right, my love?"

"Yes ... I ..."

But the door had half closed.

The man unwrapped his fish and chips, tore off a large chunk of fish with his thick work-hardened fingers and stuffed it into his mouth.

"I tol' 'im," he said indistinctly, "I tol' 'im to beware of them, I did."

"Beware of whom?"

The man stopped chewing and swallowed. "The Shinies!"

The side door was flung open with such force it banged against the wall behind it.

"That's enough of your nonsense! Out!"

"But I only ..."

The woman pointed toward the street door, "Out!"

"But I was only ..."

"Do you want me to get Bob?"

The man mumbled something, folded up his food roughly in its paper and got up. But as he squeezed past Sue he whispered, "Din't mean no 'arm. Bu' now e's gone."

Sue could feel her heart thumping painfully.

The woman came in, wiping her hands on her apron and sat down in front of her. "Sorry about that. He gets these weird ideas. You're sure you're all right?"

Sue nodded. Anything but.

"Just get you a cup of tea, okay, love?"

"Oh, thank you. That would be lovely." She would be glad of a chance to talk, even though she was sure the tea would be awful.

The door stayed open and she thought she could hear the sound of swishing and clanking, but no voices. Perhaps they had already packed up. She looked at her watch – nine already!

The woman came back with a mug of tea so brown you could stand your spoon in it. Sue hated strong tea, but it might get rid of the oil on the roof of her mouth. What she really wanted was information.

"We're closed now. I must apologise for Jeff. We all tolerate him because it was so sad about his wife dying – but it must be a bit frightening for outsiders."

"No, it's really all right. My name's Sue by the way. Thanks for the tea," She took a gulp. Yuck.

"I'm Gwen. Where you from, Sue?"

"Birmingham."

"S' long way. Stayin' long?"

"I don't know – I'm looking for someone. About five six, pale blue eyes, thinning hair, bit of a shabby dresser."

"Doesn't ring any bells – sorry. How long has he been here then?"

"Only a couple of days I think."

"A man moved into Hywell Jones's house up by the cliff. Wun't sell f'rages. People said it was 'aunted."

"Haunted?" Sue suppressed a laugh.

The woman put a finger to her lips, got up and closed the door. She sat down again and put her hands on Sue's. She looked serious.

"Person'lly I don' believe it – but there's them that do," she said quietly. "Bes' not mention how y' feel."

"What are the Shinies?"

The woman looked from left to right. Her voice sank to a whisper. "Just somethin' Jeff's got a bee in his bonnet about. Bes' leave it alone eh?" She patted Sue's hand and made to get up.

"Where is Jones's old house?"

"Full of questions ar'n't yer?" – but she said it with a smile. "On the front, juss pars the lifeboat station. Pale green paint, sash windows, yard in front. But I wouldn't go there …"

Over and over again she felt she was coming up against a brick wall – not just a wall, but one with razor wire and watchtowers on top.

"Well, thanks very much. I hope I'll see you again."

"I'd like that. But I'd get back to the Dysons' – after all – '*It's late in the season*'!" they chorused and giggled.

"Good night, love. Take care of yourself."

"I will."

Sue got up and wondered whether she should shake hands, but that might seem weird.

Suddenly, the woman leant forward and kissed her on the cheek – then turned away quickly and went back into the shop.

Sue let herself out into the street. She sensed the woman was torn between spilling the beans and keeping silent.

The wind cut through her. It would be nice to return to the quiet, possibly warm room. But …

She couldn't sleep without at least seeing if he was in.

The village street curved gently along the bay.

She felt terribly alone with only the sea for company, breathing in and out behind the houses.

She pressed on, pulling up her collar and stuffing her hands into her pockets. All the time she felt someone or something was watching her.

Further down the houses were larger and more well-to-do – some double fronted, some pebble dashed or plain red brick faced.

Ahead was a shop, standing on a corner of a road that stretched away to the left and a lane backed by houses that faced a road fronting the sea.

There was the lifeboat station, on her right, and beyond it, on the same side, a narrow parking space for boats behind the low sea wall. They were packed in, side by side, like sardines.

She must be nearly there.

She crossed over the road and walked along the path next to the boat yard looking to her left.

There it was.

In the middle of the peeling door was a discoloured brass door knocker. Light shone dully on it from the road. A dirty low wall stood in front of the glistening crazy paved yard behind which stood a decrepit semi with peeling green paint and sash windows. A dark entry separated it from the next house on the left. There was a light in the front room in the other half of the semi to the right, but Alistair's house was dark.

Perhaps he had gone to bed. But it was only 9.15. A bit early for that. Sue went through the gateless opening in the wall and down a slope to the side porch.

So intent was she on seeing whether he was in she failed to notice that her friendship ring, the twin of the one she had given to Alistair, had grown warm and then gave her a slight twinge.

In the middle of the peeling door was a discoloured brass door knocker. Light shone on it from the road.

A blast of wind blew past down the entry as she stretched out her hand and grasped it.

Immediately a shock ran up her arm and into her brain. She staggered back with a scream, shaking her head vigorously.

Was this some hideous anti-burglar device? The house loomed over her against the sky scudding with cloud.

Light from the left, through the glass in the front door side on to her, abruptly came on. It opened and a cross middle-aged face looked out.

"What the hell's going on?"

"That knocker's lethal."

"So don't touch it then!"

"I was looking for someone."

"Who?"

"The man who owns this house."

"Oh, don't know. Haven't seen him. They say he's called Alistair or something. Look I'm getting cold. Good night." The door closed abruptly and the light shut off.

Helpful round here, aren't they? she thought. Maybe he was in the back. She took a couple of steps past the porch –

Her foot plunged into empty space.

Chapter 7

Sue fell heavily.

For a moment all was darkness. Then she found herself lying downhill on her back, staring up at the sky. Dimly seen clouds swept by overhead and the moon came out fitfully. The house seemed to look down on her.

She struggled to get up, but couldn't. Her head throbbed and her shoulder was agony. She found she was crying – hot tears of fear and frustration coursed down her cheeks.

She was lying next to a rusting green drainpipe. She grasped it and struggled to sit up. On the third attempt she managed to drag herself up with a huge effort, grasping the rough gritty surface and climbing up it.

Next thing, try and drag yourself right up. She took a firm grip. 1, 2, 3, heave! God that hurt! She clung on giddily as the world spun. Felt sick.

She looked down and could see in deep shadow the high step she had just fallen down.

She stood there clinging to the pipe, waves of pain pulsing through her. She grabbed onto the next drainpipe by the side of the porch and breathed in and out slowly.

Right foot forward and up and the next one. She was up the step. Chuffing Nora!

Now to make it across the gap to next door's drainpipe by the porch. Big breaths. Go!

She reached the door and leant against the bell push.

After what seemed an age the door opened. The man put his head out. "You again? Whatcherwant?"

"Fell down the entry."

"So?"

"Hurt my shoulder. Rather badly." The world swam and she began to fall.

"Orlright. I got yer. You berrer come inside."

She felt a strong arm underneath her right arm and she was lifted like a ragdoll into a dimly lit hall and sat on a hard chair.

The man dialled a number on the phone on the hall table next to the mirror opposite her. God, she looked awful! She could just make out her fuzzy self – pale with great black blotches under her eyes … and where had her glasses gone?

"Ambulance, please." The man looked down, "They want to know how you feel."

"Bloody awful."

"She fell … Yeah. Down the entry between my house and next door … Here, Miss, you tell 'em."

Sue did her best to explain and gave him back the phone.

"They say they'll be 'ere in 15 minutes."

"Thanks".

"I'll get you some painkillers."

"Could you find my glasses?"

"Okay. I'll just gerrer a torch."

When he handed them back to her one lens was cracked and a wing was bent. She put them on nevertheless.

She had just downed a glass of something evil and fizzing when there was a screech and she could see orange light flickering through the half glazed door.

The bell sounded and the man pulled open the door. A bald young paramedic came in and stood over her. She could hear the sound of radio chatter behind him.

"What you been up to, love?"

"Fell in the entry."

"What did you give her?" he said, noticing the glass she was still holding.

"Co-codamol."

The man winced. "Okay, love. I'm Dave and you're?"

"Sue."

"Right Sue. Where does it hurt?"

"My left shoulder and back – and my head hurts like …"

"Do you think you can walk if I support you?"

"I don't know," she said. Her voice sounded small and tired.

"Okay. Right. Mike, can you get the chair?" he said to another, older man who was standing at the door. "It's not far. Sure you're all right?"

"Yes." It was a whisper.

Mike handed the canvas folding chair through the door and Sue carefully slid sideways off the hall chair into it.

"Right. Lift. Mind the threshold. Down a step. Good. Right. Nice and slowly."

Together the two men made progress up the slope through the gate and up the ramp into the back of the ambulance. Once inside she slid onto the bed.

"Can you lie down for me, Sue? You'll be much safer that way."

Dave strapped her in and sat down beside her. He got a clipboard out and started taking down details – but in the middle she fell asleep.

When she woke up she could see the dark shapes of hedgerows whizzing past.

"Sorry – think I'm going to be sick."

Dave just got a cardboard bowl under her chin before her supper came up.

After she thought she'd brought up the soles of her boots he wiped her mouth tenderly with a dark green paper towel.

"Won't be long now. Funny that," he said half to himself, "People really seem to be accident-prone round that house."

The ambulance drew up on the apron of the hospital underneath an overhanging roof. Light rain began to fall, backlit by the hospital lights.

Mike went inside and got a wheelchair and Dave slowly pushed her down the ramp and onto the tarmac. The hospital doors slid open and they were inside, turning right into a quiet waiting area where she was left while they reported in a few feet away.

A couple of nurses came out of a windowed 'glasshouse' nearby. "Can you get up?" asked one.

"Can you help?"

They helped her onto a bed as the two ambulancemen came over and she waved goodbye to them faintly.

Later she was wheeled into x-ray and a monster camera rolled noisily across the roof and descended.

"How do you feel?" A nurse asked when she was taken back to A. & E.

"'Hurts like hell."

"I'd give you some painkillers, but you've already had some. I think the doctor should see you first. Shouldn't be long."

She lay there looking at the ceiling. Her vision clouded and she was standing in a large old-fashioned wood panelled room. A woman with grey hair was staring at her with eyes that were full of darkness. She stretched out her hand –

"Sue Masters?"

The vision shut off. A man in a white coat was looking down at her. "Yes," she whispered.

"What's your date of birth?"

"And your address?"

She gave it.

"How long am I going to be here?"

"We don't know until we've seen the x-rays. Why – is there something you need to do?"

"I have to be back in Birmingham by Monday."

The doctor looked at her searchingly. "No chance of that I'm afraid."

"But …"

"It's no good getting excited. We don't know what you've done to yourself. You may have concussion. I'll arrange for the nurse to bring you some different painkillers. Try and sleep and someone will see you in the morning. We'll get you into a ward as soon as we can."

He strode off, parting the curtains around her bed as he went. After what seemed an age a nurse entered and handed her a little disposable cardboard cup with two white pills and two red pills in it. She took them obediently, too tired to even ask what they were.

She dropped into a deep sleep.

But not dreamless.

Red and black snakes writhed ceaselessly over a woman's naked body. She turned round and looked at her with eyes that were pools of night.

Chapter 8

Somehow he had fallen asleep and the daylight had not woken him, even though the curtains were not drawn.

During the night he must have pulled the blankets over his head and he woke up sweating with a head like lead.

Yesterday had been an exhausting day – and then there had been all that terrifying stuff last night. Had it all happened? He was sure it had.

He looked at his watch. 10 o'clock. Where had the day gone?

The sky was overcast with the threat of rain.

He couldn't even remember what day it was.

He got up and looked blearily in the mirror over the basin in the corner. The silvering was perishing and black holes punctured his image – an image of a tramp. Hair all over the place, two days' worth of stubble at least. Bloodshot eyes. Hardly an answer to a maiden's prayer.

The cold water tap coughed twice and then a thin spittle of liquid slithered into the dusty bowl as he turned it on. He twisted the tap to full on but it wasn't much better. He rubbed his face with his hands in what water there was.

The first thing to do would be to have a bath. At least he could depend on the water heater having come on overnight on the off-peak rate, couldn't he?

After a lot of water hammer the hot tap disgorged warmish water into the chipped enamel bath on claw feet.

He threw off his clothes and plunged in.

It was better than nothing, and it did eventually make him feel better after he'd worked up a lather.

He approached the front bedroom with caution, but there was nothing. No feeling of foreboding at all – in fact the sun was breaking through the clouds at the back of the house and shone through the doors into the room lighting up how drab and dusty it was.

He got some new clothes out of a suitcase, scrubbed his teeth and went downstairs

The sitting room door was closed, its brown paint veined and cracked. Funny, he didn't remember closing it.

He turned the knob tentatively, even afraid he might get a shock off it and peered inside. The light was off. So was the fire. And the radio. It was if nothing had ever happened.

But it had. He was sure of it. It just didn't make any sense.

He went into the kitchen, made some tea and some toast in the ancient toaster, which looked like it could blow up at any minute. Who had three pin round plugs anymore? This place could be a death trap. No wonder it was so cheap. He was going to have to spend a lot of money on it – money he couldn't afford.

He sat at the kitchen table, staring out of the window into the concrete yard and the lane beyond, bounded by a hedge from behind which the roofs of caravans poked. The hills beyond were scattered with slow moving shadows as the watery sun came and went.

Could he have imagined it all? Gone to sleep in a chair and dreamt it all?

He phoned John.

"Yes, what is it?" was the tetchy reply.

"Did I phone you last night?"

"Sure did. You were rambling on and on."

"Sorry about that."

"Yeah. Well. I'd say you'd been at the booze, except that you don't drink."

"What time was it?"

"Oh, I dunno. About 11.15. You did sound very sleepy."

"11.15!"

"Yes. Something wrong with that?"

"Not about 9.30?"

"No. Definitely. It was right in the middle of some awful panel show. Don't know why I watch such tripe."

Alistair remembered the canned laughter. "Sorry to bother you."

"It's okay. You take care, okay?"

"What was that about Sue?"

"Sue?"

"Sue Masters. You said she was coming."

"Oh, did I? Oh sorry. Just trying to cheer you up. She did ask where you were. Look, if it's all same to you, got to go okay? Bye."

He had to know. He strode back into the sitting room, picked up the TV supplement and scanned the listings for Saturday night.

There it was: Channel 4. *Penny Falls Unplugged* 11 o'clock. Really post-watershed.

What was going on?

Absently he ran his hand over his chin and discovered again the roughness of it. Couldn't go out like that to get a paper.

After shaving and a hair brush he felt a bit more respectable. He needn't have bothered. At the corner shop they 'served' him without a glance.

He came back with a plan for the rest of the day – quick read of the headlines, lunch and then tackle the hall.

Lunch was uninspiring – tinned mushroom soup with added mushrooms, an omelette and a banana. Now to get on. He went into the hall.

An old-fashioned stair carpet went up the middle of the wooden staircase, brown paint on either side of it. It was held in position by brass stair rods with large ornamental headed screws in the shape of flower heads. Black and dusty it was obvious they hadn't been polished for years. Before he could do any painting they'd have to come off.

He went upstairs and changed into some old clothes and came back down to the bottom. He bent down to unscrew the first rod and felt a faint tingling in his hand. The further he unscrewed it the stronger the feeling became until, at last, he got it off. But he wasn't going to be deterred. Probably due to the coldness and roughness of the metal.

But the moment he began to unscrew the other end the effect was instantaneous – like an electric shock. He opened his hand with difficulty. In the centre of his palm was the brown imprint of the flower. It burned like crazy.

What did you do about burns? He didn't know. Only that you had to do something pronto. Perhaps Angharad would know.

He ran into the kitchen, wrenched open the door with his other hand – and tripped over the sill.

The next thing he knew he was juddering down the steps on his front into the yard, hands and arms scraping painfully on the way.

He heard a car door open and steps in the yard.

"You all right?"

He had to squeeze the word out – "No."

"Try and sit up."

He did so and promptly vomited.

The man moved away and spoke into his mobile phone. Alistair couldn't hear what he said.

"They can't get an ambulance out for half an hour. I'd better take you to the hospital myself."

The man put his arm under Alistair's armpit and heaved him to his feet. He felt he was being kidnapped rather than helped.

"Stop, will you? I don't know who you are."

"Someone who only wishes you well. I think you've got concussion."

He found himself half lifted, half dragged across the yard and propped against the car while the man opened the passenger door. He was pushed inside.

With a squeal of tyres the car took off.

He blacked out.

He came to with hedges flashing past. His head ached.

"Is it far to the hospital?"

"Not far."

The light was failing – soon it would be dark – but even in his state it didn't look like the way to Traethmor. He looked blearily at his watch.

Fifteen minutes later he was sure. As the man turned the wheel, the left hand sleeve of his shirt slipped down, exposing a half-moon surrounded by stars. He didn't like it.

"Stop this car!" His voice sounded distant.

The man didn't answer, but trod heavily on the accelerator.

There were voices in his head, all speaking together like a badly tuned radio. One voice stood out – the female voice in his dream – he was sure of it. "I saw him first. Don't trust this man. He will take you away from us."

The car was slowing down for a sharp bend. He grabbed the handbrake and yanked it hard, ignoring the pain in his hand.

The car slewed across the road, hit the high bank on the right and stopped dead.

An airbag exploded, pinning the driver to his seat. The man looked too shocked to move.

Surprised that the one in front of him had failed to go off and only slightly wrenched by the seatbelt, Alistair unclipped it and reached for the door. The man tried to squeeze round to him, but was held fast by the bag. Why didn't it deflate?

Not pushing his luck he lurched out the car. Rain began to fall. The car's headlights provided just enough illumination to see a half-rotted gate partially open to his left. He squeezed through the gap and squatted down behind the hedge.

Chapter 9

The rain became heavier, blotting out his hearing as it hit the hedge and the surrounding greenery.

Should he make a move? He looked to his left. Far off he thought he could see a light.

His erstwhile captor could get free or otherwise summon help. In any case he couldn't stay here.

He got up, stretched his aching joints. His hand still hurt and his chest wasn't too good. Better take it slowly.

The field was of stubble and really scratchy. It occasionally nearly tripped him up. The rain began to lessen, but he was soaked through. He tried not to sneeze just in case someone was still around.

Reaching the end of the field he came across a thorn hedge. He followed it, hoping for a gap as it was taking him away from the light.

Just when it seemed to be going on forever he made out a stile beside a gate. He mounted it with difficulty as the wood was slimy with mould and rain.

The moon emerged showing grey stubbly grass. The light was now to his right and he made towards it, only to find his way blocked by a ditch full of water reflected in the moonlight. Over the hedge he could see that the light was coming from French windows to what could be a sitting-room.

He followed the ditch along and passed the dark bulk of the side of the house. Here the ditch went under a culvert and he came up against another hedge.

By now his feet were freezing from the mud oozing through his shoes as he looked for a gap.

A car's headlights far to his left momentarily outlined a gate onto a road which gave him renewed heart.

The gate was covered in cold slimy mould and difficult to get over. He fell rather than dismounted on the other side, finding himself on potholed tarmac which glimmered in the moonlight.

Hobbling up the road he came to a gate to the house behind which was a gravelled drive.

The gate was stiff, but he was in, scrunching towards the house – a Victorian looking gabled affair with dead and dying creeper clinging to its yellow brick.

He mounted the crumbling stone steps to the porch and a security light momentarily blinded him.

He pressed an old-fashioned white bell push and waited.

After a minute or so he heard slow footsteps flapping against what could be tiles. The door slowly opened on a chain. Very dim light shone out and a head peered out at him, the face in shadow.

"Yes?" The voice was tremulous.

"I'm lost."

"Well, what do you expect me to do about it?"

"Tell me where I am?"

"Not sure. Where are you heading?"

"Pen Y Bont"

"Oh, you're miles away. Have you got a map?"

"Look could I come in a minute? I'm soaked through and it's cold."

"Well, I dunno." The head thrust forward. He could see an old, bent woman with a shawl over her head. She peered at him from behind horn rimmed glasses. "What's your name?"

"Alistair."

"Hmm. Knew an Alistair once. Didn't like him. You're not him are you?"

"No, I don't think so."

"Oh, well, you seem harmless enough." He heard the sound of the chain unhooking.

The door opened onto a high ceilinged tiled hall that vanished into the darkness on either side. Light spilled from a door at the other end.

He came in and she pushed the door closed. "Better take those shoes off and those socks. I'll fetch a towel."

She waddled off slowly towards the light. By the time he got his shoes and socks off she was back.

"Sit down on that chair."

She handed him a threadbare towel and he got most of the mud off. The floor was freezing to his naked feet.

"Come on in, get yourself warm."

He followed her into a book lined sitting room with a blazing log fire.

The old lady drew the curtains and straightened up, pulling off her shawl and taking off her glasses. Although her hair was grey she was surprisingly tall and hardly bent at all. She looked at him keenly.

"Tea?"

"Yes, thanks. Weak, no sugar."

"Oh, I think you should have some sugar. You've had quite a shock."

"How do you know?"

The blue eyes regarding him knowingly and she gave the hint of a smile. "Sit down, young man. You're making the place look untidy."

She seemed to be gone a long time and he fell into a half doze beside the fire.

"You've come a long way across several fields. Why was that I wonder?"

"What?"

"Doesn't take a great detective to work that one out. Pen-Y-Bont is just down the road – well signposted, so what's the story?"

"I ran away."

"Uh-huh," she said handed him the tea. "Thought as much."

"Someone tried to kidnap me."

She sat down opposite him in a high backed chair and steepled her fingers under her nose.

"Hmm. Sounds like one of my plots."

She looked strangely familiar, but older. She picked up a book from a low table next to her chair and handed it to him. The cover was of a dark house with a man running away from it. "Saxby Close." He turned it over. The picture on the back clinched it. "You're Stephanie Chambers!"

She nodded. "Still no golden dagger, the gits," she said. "I'll never win the Booker, but I sure shift a lot of books."

"Well, I never!"

"So you have heard of me then?"

"Of course. Sorry-never read any, though. Detective fiction's not my thing."

"Ah well. Least you're honest. You'd better get out of those wet things. I'll get you some of my husband's. He was about your size."

She got up and waddled off. While she was gone he inspected some of her bookshelves. Certainly an eclectic lot. Her detective novels – of course – but books on history, archaeology, botany …

"Here you are."

He looked round guiltily.

"Oh, it's all right. I don't keep the really good stuff on show." She smiled and handed him a pile of clothing. "Like something to eat? Then we'll talk. Soup and a roll do for now?"

"That would be great."

She got back sooner than expected, but not before he had got a shirt and trousers on. She handed him a tray.

"Now, how does a young man come to be wandering about the countryside on a night like this I wonder?"

"I've just bought a house in Aberceldy. I want to renovate it, but no one wants to help. Neither does the house."

Ms. Chambers folded her hands in her lap and looked gravely at him. "You have to be careful with some houses. They don't like being mucked about with. Take this one for instance. You have to proceed very slowly. It may look decrepit and olde worlde but … Anyway I think it likes books."

"You're sending me up!"

"Certainly not. There are more things in heaven and earth …"

"Than are dreamt of in your philosophy," he said, completing the quote.

She smiled wintrily. "Perhaps."

"I tripped over the door frame and fell down the back steps after I got a shock off a stair rod. Next minute a man is whisking me off in his car, saying he's taking me to hospital."

"And wasn't he?"

"Is there one round here?"

"Go on."

"Just as he was slowing down for a tight bend I pulled on the handbrake, the car slid into a bank and the airbag exploded, pinning him to his seat. I ran across the fields."

"And ended up here?"

"That's about it."

The doorbell rang, making him jump. Stephanie Chambers got to her feet, put on the horn-rims, pulled on the shawl, adopted a stooped pose and left the room, pulling the door behind her.

He heard the front door open and muttered conversation. Then the door closed again. She came back in, shut the door and took off her glasses.

"They're looking for you."

"What did you say?"

"Hadn't seen anybody all day. Sorry about the old lady pose. Gets rid of undesirables while enabling me to size them up."

"Thanks."

"Show me your hand."

With everything that had been going on he had nearly forgotten about it. He opened it up and she took it in hers. He thought she whispered something under her breath, traced the surface slowly and then looked up. "Hmm. Most interesting"

She went over to the bookcase and pulled out a large leather bound volume with a ribbed lateral spine. It opened with a crackling sound.

She sat down, looked at the index and turned to a page.

"Hah!"

"What?"

"*Cygnosia officianale* or Hounds Tongue. Inspector Carnforth traced it down because of its musty smell."

"Oh."

"Not very well read are you? Ah, such is fame!" She looked keenly at him. "Have you been having any visions?"

Alistair was stunned. "Where?"

"In your house."

"Yes, I have as a matter of fact. How do you ..."

"Uh-huh. Know anything about the man who owned it before you?"

"No, nothing."

She tapped a finger against her lips and closed the book with a snap.

"What you know about The Greys?" He asked, worrying what the answer might be.

She looked up sharply "Don't you go getting mixed up with them, young man."

"Everybody seems rather wound up about them."

"Everybody?" She looked at him piercingly.

"There was this bloke in a pub and his sister … long story."

Her face winced. "Some people call them nutters, some people think they're onto something. Whatever they are, they're dangerous."

'*I wish I hadn't started this conversation now*', he thought – sometimes it's better not to know. Too late now …

"In what way dangerous?"

"They're trying to communicate with other worlds."

"Oh, just nutters then."

"You don't believe that."

"Why?"

"It was the way you said it. You like to tell me about it?"

"Tell you about what?"

"What you saw!"

"I didn't see anything – except a football kicked against the kitchen window."

Her lips thinned. "Hear anything?"

"Now you're going to think I'm a nutter."

"On the contrary, you're as sane as I am. So …"

"I went to sleep in the sitting room. Woke up as cold as ice. Put the fire on. Later, when I went to turn it off there was this storm in my head."

"And?"

"They said not to."

"Why?"

"They said 'We're so cold'."

She pursed her lips. "The Ninth or Frozen Circle"

"What?!"

"Don't worry. Just theorising."

"Don't worry!" He was half out of his chair.

"Anything else?"

He sat down slowly. "There was this female voice. 'We must take care of him. He's the first one for years'."

Several emotions chased quickly over Ms Chambers's face. She sat back in her chair. "You mustn't go back there unless you're properly prepared. Better not go at all."

"But …"

"I think she doesn't mean you any harm. But it's The Greys I'm worried about." She took her glasses off and tapped them against her teeth. "Well, it's getting late. Time for bed."

"You think I'm going to sleep now after all you've told me and worse – hinted at?"

She smiled. "Don't worry – you're perfectly safe here. I really should keep my thoughts to myself and not go round frightening people. I shall begin to believe what they say about me."

"What's that?"

"Round here they call me *Y bonddiges llwyd* – the Grey Lady. I'm a white witch."

Chapter 10

Sue woke up sweating to the sound of a hospital day in full swing. She looked at her watch. 7.30 in the morning. Change over time. But what day was it? She was confused. The horrible gown they'd dressed her in at some stage was itchy.

Somewhere a mobile was trilling. She sat up and pain bit into her shoulder even through the drugs. She dropped back.

The mobile went on and on. She opened her bedside cupboard despite the pain. The sound became louder. Someone had thoughtfully put it on the top shelf inside. Just as she picked it up it stopped. One missed call from John. She must call him back.

"John Hunter."

"John, it's me," she whispered.

"Hello me. Where are you?"

"Wales."

"You didn't!"

"I did."

"Idiot!" She couldn't tell whether there was genuine anger or a laugh in his voice. "Have you found him?"

"No. Fell down the entry in the dark by his house."

"And?"

"I'm in hospital."

"Shit! What have you done to yourself?" he asked wearily.

"Hurt my shoulder and hip. Hurts like buggery."

"Language, young lady! So what am I going to do about tomorrow?"

"Tomorrow?" she said, vaguely.

"Tomorrow's Monday. Are you all right Sue?"

"You mean today's Sunday?"

"All day."

"Oh, get Marilyn to do it. "

"On annual leave."

"Well, get her off annual bloody leave! Ow! Bloody shoulder! This is an emergency!"

"Yup. S'pose so. I oughta come down and get you."

"Before a major trial? Don't be daft!"

The curtains whisked back and a nurse glowered at her. "What's all this noise?"

"Sorry. Got to go. Think I'm causing a disturbance." She turned the phone off and looked at the nurse with a 'Yes?' expression.

"There are some seriously ill people here, you know"

"Sorry. That was the boss. Me being here is a major problem. Have they found what was wrong with me yet?"

"The doctor will be doing his rounds in about a couple of hours. What would you like for breakfast?"

"What is there?"

"Cereal and toast. You weren't here yesterday to sign the form."

"Can I have some more painkillers?"

"Sorry. Have to wait till the doctor comes."

Sue sank back with a sigh.

"But we should be able to get you onto a proper ward today."

Great! She felt she was being sucked into a machine and would never see daylight again.

*****

Having had a CT scan on her head which she didn't like much – even partial enclosure made her feel claustrophobic – Sue now found herself on a ward. This was a definite improvement in one way in that the mattress was a good deal more comfortable, but not in other ways. She was now in another one of those horrible cotton smocks tied at the back and very draughty and they still hadn't told her what was wrong with her.

She was staring at the black globe suspended from the ceiling above the curtains when they were whisked back and a doctor came in.

"Can you tell me your name please? … Thank you. And your date of birth? … Fine … And your address? … Well, we've had a look at the x-rays and the scan and I'm pleased to tell you that there's no internal bleeding and no bones broken … But you've seriously bruised your shoulder and hip. I think we better keep you in for a bit for observation."

"When can I go home?"

"That's a difficult one. You may have concussion. You live a fair distance away. Is there anyone who can come and pick you up?"

"No – not really."

"No parents, relatives, boyfriend even, to look after you once you get home?"

"My mother died three years ago. My nearest relative lives in Northumberland. I haven't got a boyfriend."

"Pity." He pursed his lips." Maybe Tuesday."

"But …"

"No buts, Miss? er, Masters. Ah, here comes the nurse with more painkillers and to take your blood pressure." And with that he disappeared through the curtains.

Sue subjected herself to another blood pressure test. She had lost count of how many they had taken even – even waking her up in the middle of the night. And the blood tests. They were certainly thorough – she'd give them that.

Once the pills began to work she drifted off into a haze.

The was a coolness in her brain. That was nice. Something calmed her fears and made her pleasantly relaxed. She felt herself smiling and opened her eyes to find herself looking into emerald ones set in a middle-aged face framed by grey hair.

"There, that's much better," the lady said, moving out of her frame of vision. She heard a chair grate and squeak across the floor. Turning her head she saw the woman sitting beside her. She looked a bit like Madam Arcati out of *Blithe Spirit*. Then she felt her hand held and coolness spread up her arm.

"So, what were you doing at the house?"

Sue immediately withdrew her hand and was instantly wary. "What house?"

"His house."

"I don't know what you're talking about!"

"Alistair stayed with me last night. He is a disturbed young man. But that's not surprising, given the circumstances."

Sue decided to drop all pretence. "So you've seen him?"

"Yes. As I said. But I should leave him alone if I were you. Go back to Birmingham. He's got enough problems without you."

"What right have you to interfere? Who are you?"

"Someone you wouldn't like to upset."

Then realisation suddenly hit her. "You were in my dream. You're evil! Nurse!"

There was a pad of footsteps and the curtains were thrown open. "What's going on here? Are you annoying this patient?"

"No. No. I was just going." The woman patted Sue's cheek, but not affectionately. "Remember what I said." And left.

"Who was that?" asked Sue

"Someone who said she knew you and you said you hadn't got anyone down here and I thought it would be nice for you to have someone to chat to."

"That was kind of you. But please don't let her in again."

"Why ever not?"

Sue thought fast. Any explanation would sound weird. "She's just not my favourite person."

"Ok, ok."

As soon as the nurse had gone she reached for her mobile and phoned her boss again.

"John? It's me again."

"And?"

"Just had this strange experience. It's really made me angry."

"What?"

"This strange woman looking like a reject from a fortune-telling tent on the pier has just warned me off finding Alistair."

"So you know where he is?"

"I know where he was."

"Go on."

"With this strange woman last night or maybe early this morning – I'm confused …"

"A woman you say? Stone me!"

Knowing that it took a lot to surprise John she listened for the next bit. "If I know anything about you, that will make you even more determined."

"Too right. I just wish they'd let me out of here."

"So have they said what's wrong?"

"No broken bones, no internal bleeding, but a lot of bruising."

"Hmm. I wouldn't go chasing after him yet then. Sounds like you've had a nasty fall. Not going to do you any good charging about the place."

"I know, but –"

"But me no buts, madam. I'm sure they know what's best for you. Got someone lined up to take notes in court tomorrow – so not to worry, okay? You just get better."

"I don't think this woman's good news. And he's just come out of a relationship. He's very vulnerable."

"Can I hear just a hint of jealousy?"

"It's difficult being friends with both Liz and Alistair."
"I know." She heard John sigh. "You do pick 'em, don't you?"
Sue breathed in hard.
"You know how to give a girl a good time don't you?"
"Just speaking the truth. See you soon, okay?"
"You think I should come back?"
"Only you can decide that. The world won't crumble. I'll still be here. You look after yourself and don't do anything silly, okay?"
"I don't know about that. But thanks anyway. Bye."
He was a lot older than her. Perhaps he did know best. She put the phone back on the locker and lay back, staring at the ceiling. Perhaps he was right. Perhaps she was jealous. She'd given Alistair that Friendship Ring after all.

She urgently needed to pee.

Carefully she raised herself up and sat on the edge of the bed. Then, supporting herself on the bedside cabinet she stood up. Gosh, the floor was cold!

All right so far. Just. She tried a few steps forward. A bit dizzy maybe but …

"What are you doing out of bed?" a passing nurse demanded.
"Need to go to the loo."
"I'll bring you a bedpan."
"No … I."

The nurse looked exasperated.

Sue turned round unsteadily and got back into bed.

It was a very long morning and even longer afternoon.

Nothing to do but stare at the ceiling. Visitors came and went. Apart from a large Jamaican lady who delivered her breakfast and lunch (if you could call it that) who paused for a brief chat the hospital ignored her.

I've got to get out of here. Must.

Can't go back to Birmingham. I've got to find him. Must find him.

She fell asleep from boredom as the light level dropped steadily behind the windows into evening and then, imperceptibly into night.

*****

Sue came to be gradually aware of people bustling about behind the curtains surrounding her bed.

The doctor came in breezily, slipping in between them with an attendant nurse.

"Good morning, Miss Masters. Did you sleep well?"

"As much as one can in a hospital."

"Yerrs. Now I'm going to shine a light into your eyes. Try and keep them open … Aha … How many fingers am I holding up?"

"Three."

"Good."

He produced an optician's page the size of a paperback with paragraphs in different size fonts. "Can you read the second paragraph for me?"

"I need my glasses." She turned over and opened the drawer in the bedside table wincing with the pain. She put them on.

"Out loud, if you please."

She did so.

"Perfect."

"Could you stand up for me?"

Sue got up slowly and a bit unsteadily. The nurse looked ready to pounce if anything was amiss. She didn't feel too bad – but the floor was freezing.

"Now close your eyes." Sue wobbled slightly. "Now open them. Good. Stretch out your right arm and touch the tip of your nose with the tip of your right index finger … Perfect. Right. Put your clothes on and I'll be back soon."

"What day is it?"

"Monday." And he was gone. The nurse raised an eyebrow, gave her a half smile and then she was gone too.

Sue slowly got into her clothes from her locker. She felt a little giddy, but she was determined to get out. Nothing was going to stop her.

He was a long time coming back. She sat in the high backed chair next to the bed and stared at the closed curtains until the pattern was beginning to send her boss-eyed.

When he eventually came back he got her to go up a flight of stairs in the hall the end of the ward. At first they looked like the north face of Everest, but after initial giddiness she got used to it. Coming down was slightly worse, but she hung onto the balustrade grimly. She was going to get out of here no matter what.

"That's fine. Well, you'll be glad to hear you can go home today. Where is home?"

"I'm on holiday at the moment so you could say The Artemis guesthouse, Aberceldy."

"Normally?"

"Birmingham. I've given my details."

"Right. Well, if you have any symptoms of giddiness, blackouts, sudden headache or nausea give us a ring okay? Bye now." And he strode off.

After collecting her shoulderbag she hung around for her discharge letter and then said goodbye to the nursing staff.

Emerging onto the hospital forecourt she was immediately buffeted by a stiff wind carrying with it the tang of salt. On coming to the pavement at the side of the road she looked downhill to see the sea in the distance.

"Where's the station?" she asked a passerby, a thin girl whose long black hair kept lashing her face.

"Down the hill, turn first left, follow the road round and it's on your left."

"Thanks."

The station was old-fashioned. None of your arcades and posh shops – just an entrance, a ticket office, waiting room and, well, nothing else. All in rather grimy chocolate brown and yellowing cream. The rusting embossed ironwork of the station name on the platform said 'Traethmor'. So that's where she was. The last stop beyond Aberceldy.

She entered the booking hall – more chocolate brown – and uncomfortable-looking bench seats. The small window to the ticket office was covered up with a board. 'Ring bell for attention', so she did.

A door banged within followed by whistling and the wood behind the glass slid up. A man opened up with a volley of Welsh. She had to bend right down to look through the glass oval cutout the man was behind. Bit antiquated, she thought.

"Single to Aberceldy, please."

"Oh right. English is it?"

"Yes." Strange, she thought, in a university town.

"Right you are, then. Right you are. That'll be two and six please."

"Sorry? Did you say two and six?"

"Yes. Anything wrong with that? It's a bargain I'd say!"

"You're asking me to pay with pre-decimal coinage?"

The man's brow creased and his mouth opened in surprise.

Sue closed their eyes and counted to 10. Everything had to be all right. It had to be. She grasped the edge of the brown ledge in front of the glass and squeezed. Then she counted to 10 again.

She opened her eyes.

She was looking at a large glass screen through which she could see the whole room. A cold shiver went down her spine and she leant on the edge of the counter for support.

"Are you all right, madam?"

She took a deep breath. It was all right. It had to be …

"How much is the fare?"

"£2.60."

Right. Get a grip now. She dug in her bag, got out a fiver and pushed it through the half circle at the bottom of the glass partition.

"You're sure you're all right, madam? You look very pale."

"I'll ... I'll ... be all right in a moment. Just got to sit down in the fresh air."

"Well, we got plenty of that," he smiled as he passed back the change.

"When's the next one due?"

The man looked up at upwards as if at a clock. "About five minutes."

"Thanks."

The roof over the platform creaked in the wind. She sat down on a hard brown slatted bench. There was nobody about.

But then, with two minutes to go, several people materialised from somewhere and stood expectantly. Somehow they looked different. Sort of fuzzy ... And those clothes –

The sound of a whistle reflected off the hills and a rattle of wheels came ever closer until, with a shrieking of brakes and a sussuration of steam an engine slowed into the station.

A *steam* engine.

Sue wanted to scream. This wasn't happening. It couldn't be happening.

But nobody seemed the least concerned. They got on quietly and began to close the doors.

"Hello, again."

She whipped round.

It was the student from her journey from Birmingham.

"You're going on this?" he asked

"I ... I ... suppose so. As far as ... as far as ... Aberceldy."

"That's great. So am I. Come on."

He held the door open for her and they got on.

Into a modern carriage.

She stopped dead. This wasn't right –

"Are you OK?" When she didn't answer he gripped her by the arm and steered her into a seat. She sat down heavily.

"Sorry about that, but you look like you were going to faint and the train was going to start and you could have fallen."

As if on cue the train jolted and started to reverse out of the station a bit and then halted. There was a shriek, a grinding of metal and then it started forwards again.

As they left the town she began to relax.

"Said I'd see you again, didn't I?" the student said.

"Have you any water?"

"Sure." He handed her a small bottle of supermarket spring water, half full. She wiped the top with her handkerchief and took a good glug.

"I think you needed that," he said as she handed it back.

She nodded, not knowing what to say. This time she had no book to hide behind.

"How do you find Aberceldy?"

"I've … hardly seen it."

The youth smiled. "Oh yes?"

"No. I've had … Had a fall. Just got out of hospital."

"Oh. Sorry to hear that. But you're all right now?"

"I … think so. Can I ask you something?"

"Ask away!"

"What's pulling us?"

He looked at her quizzically. "An engine I suppose!" He was about to laugh, but must have seen her expression. "Something bothering you?"

"What kind of engine?"

"Oh … diesel aren't they? Haven't electrified round here. Bit of a backwater in case you hadn't noticed!"

Sue pursed her lips.

"Why do you ask?"

She couldn't tell him. "I just … Can we talk about something else?"

"How'd you fall?"

"Down an entry. Missed my step in the dark. Sorry – don't want to talk about it. What are you studying?"

"Psychology."

"Oh."

"People always say 'oh', he said pleasantly. "We don't bite and we're not mind readers!"

"How … How many years have you been doing it?"

"Three years."

"And when you finish?"

"A Masters."

"You're … You'll be racking up a lot of debt."

"I s'pose."

Sue looked out the window. She wanted to get away. Go somewhere dark and get her head down. She looked her watch. It had stopped. "Can you tell me the time?"

He looked at his watch. "3:10."

"Thanks."

She wound up her watch and set the time. She couldn't bear not knowing what time it was.

He stuck his hand out. "Steve Harrison."

"Pleased to meet you, Steve." She didn't mean it. It showed in her voice.

"And you?"

"Sue. Look, if you don't mind I need to close my eyes."

"Sure."

Blessed blackness.

Then – "Aberceldy. Aberceldy station. Please collect your belongings and be careful when alighting from the train. Thank you for travelling with Cambrian Railways."

'*As if we had any choice*', she thought.

"Better get out here unless you want to go up the coast!" Steve said.

"Yes. I suppose so." She just wished he would go away. There was something about him. She didn't know what it was, but –

"I'll give you a hand."

"No, it's all right."

She half rose and he grabbed her upper arm.

"Come on. I've got you."

She wanted to scream but no one was looking. It was not their problem.

He hauled her to her feet and half dragged her out of the carriage and onto the platform.

"Let go of me!"

"Just trying to help."

"I don't … need … your … help!"

As he was pulling her the sleeve of his hoody slipped up his arm revealing something above his wrist.

Now she was sure.

"Okay. Okay." He held up his hands in mock submission. "I live up there." He pointed to a tall Victorian terrace with purple pillars next to the windows. The whole long row was painted in different hippy-like colours. It all looked so different in the daylight.

She said nothing, but pulled away from him and walked off. What was that tattoo? A crescent and three stars.

The wind blew hard as she rounded the corner, flapping some strands of hair across her glasses. A short burst of rain hit her full in the face.

And then she saw Alistair. And began to run, stumbling crazily towards him.

Chapter 11

Alistair woke in the thin light of a grey dawn. He got up and drew back the curtains. Rain ran in rivulets down the panes of a sash window.

The room smelled musty and the air was damp. He shivered.

He'd gone to bed fully clothed and had fallen into a fitful sleep, the events of the previous day replaying in his head, principally the electrocution – he looked at his hand now. The burn was already fading and it no longer hurt. A 'white witch' she'd said.

He had to get away. But where to? She said not to go back to the house. 'That house doesn't want to be painted.' It all crowded in on him until he felt he wanted to scream.

Quietly opening the bedroom door he crept out onto the landing. He wouldn't get far without any shoes. But where had she put them?

A strange odour that was both sharp and sweet stole up the stairs from the hallway.

Slowly he descended the polished wooden stairs with only a narrow strip of carpet down the middle held in place with stair rods much like in his house. His hand suddenly started to tingle. He looked down. Brass flower heads gleamed dully at the ends of the stair rods. But they were different from his.

At every creak he expected the Grey Lady to issue from one of the many downstairs doors. Though she had been friendly the night before he couldn't take that for granted.

At last he stood on the cold red quarry tiles of the hall. He could hear the downpour easily here through the glazed front door. Whatever the weather he had to go –

He stretched out his hand to the knob. It resolutely refused to budge – not a millimetre – like it was a welded shut.

Down here the smell was stronger. He looked round towards the sitting room where it seemed to be coming from and froze –

Ms Chambers was standing stark naked beyond the doorway into the sitting room with her back to him. Her surprisingly youthful body was upright. Two tattooed snakes, one red, one black, writhed, entwined, up either side of her spine, heads staring at each other, fangs bared, just below her uncoiled grey hair. Their tails curled under her bottom.

He could swear they were moving.

Her arms were out gracefully at right angles to her body. Gradually she bent backwards and swayed back and forth like a belly dancer in slow motion until she was leaning backwards from her knees at an impossible angle, staring at the ceiling.

Her eyes were pools of night.

He tried to turn away, but still he couldn't move. His eyes were drawn down to the bare floor – the carpet had been rolled back – where a pentacle had been drawn in silver, with gold candles burning in brass candlesticks at their points.

Very slowly she raised her head and torso, crossed her arms on her breasts and gave forth a great sigh, coming back slowly to the vertical. Somehow she seemed to shrink back down into herself.

"Don't just stand there, dear boy. Hand me my robe. It's just there, over that chair."

He could see a crimson silk dressing gown thrown over a high-back chair. He entered the room and handed it to her, not daring to look.

"Don't be alarmed. I know what to do now."

She turned, fastening her robe, and stepped out of the pentacle towards him, holding out an elegant hand, the fingers encrusted with chunky jewellery.

Perfumed smoke drifted away as the candles self extinguished. He looked down. Every one of them had gone out and yet there was not a puff of air in the room.

She grasped his hand and drew him to her. He smelled her hot, spicy scent. A tingle ran through him as he allowed himself to be led through a door into the kitchen.

Ms Chambers breathed in strongly and out again. "Such exercise always makes me feel ravenous. Hungry?"

Now he came to think of it he was – ravenous. But he had to get away. "Not really. Can I go now?"

"Idiot. You don't know what you're getting yourself into – but go, go." She waved her hand imperiously.

She went to the fridge and sought out a box of eggs and a pack of bacon.

"You knew that man that came last night – didn't you?" he said.

"Of course," she said, not looking at him, turning on the gas under a pan and the grill.

"And?"

She opened the vacuum pack of bacon with her teeth and laid the rashers on the grill pan, shoving them under the flames. With a practiced movement she cracked an egg with one hand.

"He was a Grey. One of the disciples."

"Disciples of what?"

"Best not to know."

"I think you're treating me like a child."

"But you are one," she said, cracking a second egg into the pan. "You won't get far without shoes. Sit down. It'll be ready soon."

He sat meekly, noticing the table was already laid for two.

"Buying a house no one will buy, tangling with forces far beyond your comprehension. Escaping by the merest good fortune."

"You wouldn't have anything to do with that, would you?" he said.

She turned, smiled wintrily and then turned off the gas. "Hold up your plate." She flipped an egg and some bacon onto it. "Eat."

"I'm really not …"

"Eat."

Between mouthfuls he said, "So what have I got myself into?"

"I've not been to the house myself, but it sounds like it exists outside time when you're in it. But not all the time. That would need tremendous amounts of temporal energy. So – only when it's necessary." She put down her knife and fork and stared distantly over his shoulder. "I wonder where it's coming from?"

"So, if I can't go back, where can I go?"

She wiped her mouth with a napkin. "Somewhere I can keep an eye on you – you've obviously been brought here for a purpose. You'd better stay at The Artemis B&B. I know the owners. I'll make a reservation while you wash up."

"But when they find out where I've gone – The Greys I mean …"

"They'll find you wherever you go. But you've burned your boats in Birmingham haven't you?"

"How the hell do you know that?"

Ms Chambers looked at him coldly. "I wouldn't use that word if I were you. It can be very dangerous."

She dug under her robe and pulled out a silver chain, unlooping it from her neck. Suspended from it was a brass half-moon.

"Put it on".

He took it. It was still warm from her skin.

"Why?"
"It will protect you."
"From what?"
"From whom."
"All right. From whom?"
"The Greys."
"How?"
"They won't be able to see you."
"What? I'll disappear?"
She sighed. "They will look for a particular aura. This will dissipate it."
He leant forward "What kind of aura?"
"You're what's called a 'Lamplighter'. They're very rare. That's why they're looking for you."
He shivered involuntarily. "That's what she said."
She looked at him sharply. "Who?"
"This voice."
Stephanie Chambers frowned. "In the house?"
"Yes."
"Where?"
"In the sitting room at the front of the house."
She compressed her lips.
"Is that bad?"
She stretched forward, took hold of his chin with a thumb and forefinger and looked deep into his eyes. Seemingly satisfied, she let go.
"Not yet."
"Not yet! What's that supposed to mean?"
"The house is a corridor. Best stay away from it. Who knows what may come through once it detects your aura … You haven't put it on."
"What? Oh, sorry." He looped it round his neck.
"Inside your clothes."

"Right." It still felt warm against his skin.

"There now. Washing up for you while I phone The Artemis." She got up in one fluid movement and went into the sitting room where he heard her dialling.

He started on the washing up. What had he got himself into? And what day was it?

"Have you finished the washing up?" Ms Chambers called from the hall. "The bus leaves soon."

"What day is it?"

She came in, fully dressed and in a white mac, half done up. "Monday of course!"

"Monday! What happened to Sunday?"

"Put you to sleep. You needed it after all the trauma you'd experience over the weekend."

"But you can't go messing about with …"

She stared at him with emerald eyes. He felt as if he had been hit by a wall.

"Your shoes," she said, "put them on. Chop! Chop! Time and Arriva wait for no man!"

He put them on.

"Is it still raining?"

"Just stopped. But I can lend you a coat of my husband's. Ready?" She handed him a black double-breasted coat and opened the front door. The moment she put the scarf over her head she bent double and adopted the duck like walk of an old crone.

Together they scrunched down the drive to an ancient Citroen 2 CV parked by the gate.

"I'll take you as far as the bus stop."

They got in. Whatever powers she had as a white witch, Alistair thought, they didn't extend to her driving. He winced every time she changed gear – it was like tearing off a rusty corrugated iron roof.

But most of all he froze. The air vents above the dashboard were fully open.

"Nothing like fresh air, dear boy," she shouted above the straining engine. "You'll get used to that around here or just learn to put up with it."

Mist was still crouching in the fields and the moisture laden air fuzzed the outline of the trees that were taking on their autumn colours.

"Here we are! Right – the bus will take you into Aberceldy alongside the sea. As soon as you see the public conveniences on your right opposite the road to your left to the station ask the driver to stop. Get off and walk the last bit so he doesn't see where you go. The Artemis is on your left. I've booked you in as David Peters. Don't forget!"

He got out and she drove off without a backward glance.

She did seem to know an alarming lot about him. What else did she know? He was glad to get away from her – but maybe she did have his best interests at heart? A chill went through him - weren't her eyes blue last night?

The bus arrived with a roar and a wheeze of air brakes, looking just as ancient and damp outside as it was in. The few passengers were muffled against cold and not a word was spoken.

As soon as he spotted the public lavatories he asked the driver to pull over. He got off by the road to the station. Why not just catch the next train out? Lack of funds, that's why. He'd only just had enough to pay the fare. You don't have much on you when you're decorating – and how on earth was he going to pay the bill?

The Artemis was an old double fronted house, its front door blocked by a board. There was nothing in the windows. He hoped it was open.

He went round the side and rang the bell. After a while he heard the slip slop of ill-fitting slippers hitting the floor behind the glazed door. A pink face surmounted by white hair in curlers looked out. "Yes?"

"I'm Al-David Peters. I've got a reservation."

She frowned. Then her face cleared. "Oh, yes, yes, yes. Come in, come in."

As he closed the door behind him a stale heat enveloped him – boiled cabbage with a hint of wet dog.

The corridor led into a small hall with stairs going up on the right by a small table with a telephone on it and a black covered book.

"Where's your luggage?" Her voice was very Welsh.

"Er – it's at a friend's at the moment. Just came to book in and look at the room."

She sniffed. "Well, I s'pose it's all right. She did say you were a bit odd."

Thanks Ms C, he thought.

"Well, she's paid for the week so … Just sign the book and I'll get you the key." She thrust it at him and went off.

He looked for a clear space … and dropped the pen. There, in her bold friendly script, was 'Sue Masters, Birmingham'. So she was here! Checked in yesterday. He picked the pen off the floor and wrote an illegible signature.

"You'll be in number six, first floor. I won't come up – my arthurrightis is something chronic today, see?"

"That's okay. This name here – Sue Masters – is she in?"

The woman looked immediately suspicious, "Why d'you want to know?"

"I know her."

The woman sniffed, pursed her lips and seemed to come to a decision. "Haven't seen her this morning. Her key's not hanging up, so I s'pose she's gone out."

"Okay, thanks."

He climbed the steep stairs, arriving slightly breathless outside number six, having noted the worn carpet that would delight the HSE boys. There might be a story in these old down-at-heel hotels.

The chipped brown painted door did not bode well and the musty smell inside the room was worse. A bed with sagging springs, a chair and a chipboard wardrobe and that was your lot. He hoped there was a bathroom nearby.

The view out of the window was over some low roofs to the railway line and beyond that, fields stretching to a church on a mound – and beyond that, hills.

He had to get clothes for a start. It was all very well Ms Chambers saying he wasn't to go back to the house – how else was he to equip himself? He couldn't even remember whether he'd locked up or not. Presumably not.

There must be a way there without going down the main street attracting attention. Perhaps there was a road or a lane leading to the church and he'd take it from there.

He crept down the stairs. A loud male voice choir was coming from somewhere which should cover his retreat.

Gaining the front door he opened it as quietly as possible and came out into the lane to his left. Closing it he breathed out heavily and set off.

As expected the lane led down to the railway line and once there he walked along a track beside it until he reached a level crossing. It was a straightforward walk down to the church. To the right a puddled lane led off round a bend which took him eventually through a farmyard and, inevitably, a dog.

It could smell his fear, he was sure of it. He didn't know what breed it was, but it was fierce, jumping up at him. Any minute he expected someone to emerge from the farmhouse, but nobody did. Eventually the dog got bored and growled off.

Another lane joined a metalled road alongside a field which had two horses in it.

While he was leaning against a post for a rest as his right ankle was paining him, one of them – a beautiful shiny chestnut with a white flash down its nose and white socks – came up to him.

He stroked its nose. "I'm sorry I haven't got anything for you."

The horse snickered and then breathed "Millie". He was sure of it. It leaned its mouth right next to his ear and breathed again – "Butters".

He started back. The horse was looking at him dead in the eye. He could see and feel the intelligence there. Backing away he tripped over a tussock of grass and fell heavily on the verge, knocking the breath out of him.

The horse snorted, shook its head and trotted off into the middle of the field where it began grazing as if nothing had happened.

This was getting too much. White witches, pentacles, talking horses …

He staggered to his feet and began walking again, looking over his shoulder occasionally. The horses continued to graze contentedly, totally uninterested in anything but what was in front of them.

The road continued on to another level crossing. Further on he could see it connected with the street running through the village. Luckily there was a track alongside the line which he followed until it veered away to pass some playing fields onto the road he had taken to Traethmor. The corner shop was up to his right. Nearly there now.

He made his back yard with a great sense of relief and staggered up the back steps.

The door was locked.

He felt in his pockets.

Nothing.

She must have taken them out. No wait a minute – he'd changed his clothes for the DIY. They must be in the house.

Perhaps Angharad was in. He couldn't stay here where he could be seen. He fingered the chain, hoping it was working its magic. He had to believe in it. What else could he do?

He knocked on her back door, straining to hear if anyone was in.

He saw her face through the panes in the half glazed door. She looked shocked as she pulled it open.

"Where have you been? Look at the state of you!"

"Long story. Can I sit down?"

"Of course. Come in, come in."

He collapsed onto a hard chair by the table. He heard her fill the kettle and put it on.

"You look like you've had quite a shock."

"Talking horses, white witches, magic – you'll never believe me!"

Her face went white and her brow furrowed. "Strong tea with lots of sugar is what you need and then a lie down in the sitting room where I can keep an eye on you."

"No. It's all right. Got to get into the house … Need things …"

"That you're not. You're in no fit state to go anywhere." She bent down and unlaced his shoes. "Have you been in a mud bath? And look at the state of your coat! Get it off this minute."

He obeyed.

The kettle boiled and switched itself off. He looked out of the window and the view began to swim.

A strong smell exploded in his head and he gasped. He opened his eyes and she was standing over him with a brown bottle.

"My husband's old smelling salts. Works every time. Had to do something to bring you round. Come on, I'll help you onto the sofa in the front room."

He allowed her to put an arm under his arm and together they lurched into a cheerful front room where the sun shone.

He collapsed onto the sofa and lay there, looking up at the white ceiling.

Presently he managed to pull himself up a bit and she came back in with a mug of tea.

"Drink that. Should help."

It was far too strong, but he drank it down gratefully. In a moment he was asleep.

When he woke up Jeff was looking at him, perched on the edge of an armchair opposite. The sun had gone down and sunset was flaming the underside of the clouds.

"You seen 'em."

"Who?"

"I can see it in your eyes."

Here we go again, he thought.

"What happened to you?" he asked.

This obviously took Jeff by surprise. "When?"

"At the pub."

"Yeah, well … You seen 'em though … The Shinies."

"Where?"

"In that house. Jones's house. You went. Didn't come back. She was worried."

Angharad came in. "Don't you go annoying him," she said, looking angrily at her brother then turning her attention to Alistair. "How you feeling?"

"Tired." He yawned.

"Where have you been? Saw you being driven away in a car. Then you didn't come back … I was worried – went into your house – the door had been left open."

"You went into the house?" He stared at her incredulously.

"Paint stuff all over and this loose stair rod lying in the hall. Nearly tripped over it I did. Picked it up and put it down on the hall chair."

"And nothing happened?"

Her brow creased. "No. It was only an old stair rod – what? Do you think anything would?"

"But it electrocuted me!"

"There! Tol' you, tol' you," Jeff said triumphantly.

"You be quiet!" she said, turning on him aggressively. "I've had a bellyful of your nonsense. Go on – make yourself useful. Get some fish and chips for us."

"But I ain't got no money!"

"Go an' get my purse, then. I know how much is in there!" she shouted after him as he left the room.

"We'll have to get you in some clean clothes. Trouble is my husband was a bigger man."

"Was?"

"Died five year ago," said Jeff coming back into the room and handing her her purse. She doled out a £10 note. "And bring me back the change!"

Jeff grumbled something under his breath and left the room. Alistair heard the back door bang.

Angharad sighed. "All right then. We'll have to go next door and get some of yours."

"But it's getting dark!"

"Will you make your flippin' mind up!" But she said it with a smile. "Are you sure you're up to it?"

He heaved himself to his feet. He felt a bit giddy, but he wasn't going to let on. "Trouble is I've been told not to."

She sat down on the arm of the chair vacated by Jeff.

"Who by?"

"An authoress called Stephanie Chambers."

"When?"

"Last night."
"You mean ... She didn't did she?"
"Didn't what?"
She rolled her eyes. "Look, you got to get used to it round here. This is not the big city where nobody knows anything ... Loads of us are related or went to school together."
"So you wouldn't place any weight on what she said?"
"Batty as a fruitcake. I can see I'm not going to get you to shut up, am I? We better go there and get back before His Highness comes back."
"Have you got a stick?"
"Sure. Still feeling a bit woozy?"
"A bit."
"Right, come on then. There's nothing wrong with your house. Needs a good clean and a spot of paint. Be as good as here."
"I doubt that."
"You'll see. I'll even come round and give you a hand if you like."
"That's extremely kind of you."
"No trouble. Done all I can do to this house. You can be my next project!"
They descended her back steps, went into the road and back into his yard.
"Was it you who locked up then?"
"Sure. Can't leave it unlocked, not these days."
The house loomed over them in the darkening sky. He stopped. "I don't know ..." He said, fingering the chain.
"Come on. How bad can it be?"
She went up the steps first and unlocked the door. He waited until she turned the light on in the kitchen and the hall and then slowly mounted the steps and went in. She had already gone upstairs.

As he went into the hall the downstairs lights went out leaving only the light coming down from upstairs. His eyes were dragged round to the circular hall mirror surrounded by copper scrollwork.

In it was a face.

A woman's face.

Her face.

Amelia Earhart.

Then it was gone. Nothing there but his own slightly distorted half lit features.

"Are you all right?" Angharad's voice, edged with concern, came from above.

He shot past the mirror, bounded up the stairs into the light, the blessed light.

"The lights went out, then I saw her face."

"Whose face?" she asked, standing in the front bedroom and looking up at him from an opened case.

"Amelia Earhart's face."

"Who's she?"

"Let's get out of here."

"Not until I've got these clothes. Once we're back next door you can tell me all about it."

He went forward to close the case – but felt too limp to lift it. She picked it up easily –

A loud bang came from downstairs. He ran into the back bedroom, but there was no one below. She ran in after him.

"Look," he said, "nobody there."

"So?"

"This happened Friday night. Come downstairs."

"I'll get the case first."

He descended the stairs slowly into the gloom and went into the unlit kitchen. She came in after him and switched on the light.

He pointed towards the window. There, on the same pane as last time was the mark of a football.

"Now do you believe me?" he said, turning towards her.

Chapter 12

When Sue got right up to him it wasn't Alistair. The man looked surprised, smiled and then the smile left his face as he realised this charming young lady running towards him with her arms outstretched wasn't for him.

"Sorry. Thought you were someone else," Sue said, going brick red.

"I'm sorry too," the man said, dipping his head and hurrying on into the wind.

What should she do now? She suddenly felt very hungry. Why not go back to that cafe? Well it was better than nothing.

She looked at her watch. 20 to 2. Wonder if they'll be open?

She walked smartly down the street to see the coloured lights were on over the apex of the roof. A sweaty warmth spilled out onto the pavement, redolent of oil and fried potato.

"Hello! Can't stay away, eh?" Gwen from last night looked up under the hot lights. "Someone from next door to Jones's just been in. That man I had to kick out last night if you remember. He wanted three portions of cod and chips. Now there's only Angharad and him at that house – so who was the third person?" Her eyes twinkled. "Could it be the man you're looking for?"

Sue went brick red again for the second time that day.

"Worth a look, eh?"

"I – er – suppose so. But I can't just go barging in there, can I?"

"Don't see why not. How about some cod and chips to cheer you up before you go? You can think about it while you're eating."

"Yes, I suppose so."

"Go on then. Large or small chips?"

"Small please."

"Hah! Not going to make my fortune outta you then!"

"'Spose not!"

Gwen grinned "There you are then," she said, wrapping it up. "You can have them next door."

Sue went through the door on her left and sat down at a small table. There were quite a few people in, all chattering away, some with young children squirming about on the hard plastic chairs.

Well, I suppose it's worth a go. He might be there. What was she going to say to him? The more she thought about it, the more embarrassing it became. She could hardly say she was 'in the area' or had 'just bumped into him'. And certainly no mention of visions. Don't want to scare him off. I don't know … I don't know … I don't know … She sighed.

She finished eating, scrunched up the paper into a ball and looked round for somewhere to put it. There wasn't anywhere. She left it on the table.

Gwen put her head round the door. "What! Still here? Good luck!"

"Thanks. Better go then."

She got up and smoothed herself down, ran her fingers through her unruly hair, realised that wasn't the most brilliant of ideas as her hair would now smell of fish, breathed in and opened the door onto the street.

A rain squall forced its way down between the houses immediately, partially blinding her. She wiped her glasses and began uncertainly to walk down the street back to the house where she had fallen down the entry. Best to approach it round the back this time.

Passing the corner shop on her left she walked slowly past the backs of the houses presenting a solid wall against the sea. It all looked so different in the light.

That must be Jones's house – and next to it the other half of the semi. A battered pale blue Austin Allegro was squeezed parallel to the lane under a rusting corrugated iron carport alongside the wall to the backyard. A flight of steps led up to the back door next to a dark green oil tank.

Opening the gate she looked up at the back of the house. Was there anybody in?

Slowly she climbed the concrete steps and knocked on a pane of glass in the half glazed door.

Nothing stirred.

She knocked again, more loudly.

Nothing.

She was about to try a third time when she saw someone come into the kitchen and head towards the door. It opened with a squeak.

A short woman in a plaid skirt, white blouse and blue cardigan stood there, her brown eyes regarding her in a noncommittal way.

"Yes?"

"I'm looking for a man about five six, 40s, called Alistair –"

"You'd better come in." She held the door wide and gestured to a hard wooden kitchen chair in front of an enamelled table in the window. "Please sit down."

"Thank you. Er – sorry don't know your name … Have you –"

"He's gone."

"Sorry?" Sue was momentarily flummoxed.

"I said he's gone."

"Gone? Gone where?"

"That's his business."

"He's not next door?"

"No."

"Sorry. We seem to have got off on the wrong foot. My name's Sue." She held out her hand. The other woman didn't take it.

"And why do you want to see him?" The eyes were searching now, beginning, maybe, to be hostile, Sue thought.

"I thought ... I thought he might be in trouble. I've ... I've come down from Birmingham."

"Have you now? Well, we don' like people coming down 'ere poking their noses into our affairs. P'rhaps you'd better go back there."

"If you see him ... would you tell him Sue's come to see him. I'm only staying another night. Would you do that for me?"

"No."

"Why not?"

"As I said. I think you better go."

Sue got up and pushed the chair under the table. She pulled a piece of paper out of her pocket and wrote on it quickly. "This is where I'm staying. If you see him ..." She tried to hand it to the woman, but when she didn't take it she left it on the table.

The woman opened the kitchen door and stood by it, watching her walk down the yard. Sue could feel her eyes boring into her back all the way out into the lane.

Where was he?

She could try his house again, she supposed.

Opening the gate to his house she looked up at it. It looked empty, unwelcoming?

This is stupid, she thought. How can a house look unwelcoming. Does a house have a soul?

She walked up the back steps and knocked on the identical half glazed door.

No answer.

She leant against the balustrade to her left and looked through the window. The kitchen looked tidy – and deserted.

A squeak to her right and the kitchen door of the semi to her right across the passageway swung open and that awful man stuck out his head.

"What? You still 'ere?"

She turned awkwardly to face him. "It would seem so."

"Well, he's norrin."

"Yes, I had worked that out for myself," she said mildly.

The door slammed shut.

"Hello!"

The voice made her jump and she nearly lost her footing. She turned round gingerly.

It was the woman from next door. She held up a key. Sue eyed her suspiciously. What was she up to?

"I thought you wanted rid of me," she said.

"I can let you in if you like. You could wait."

"Okay."

Sue descended the steps slowly and let the woman pass as she went up to open the door and went in. Sue followed. The woman went through the kitchen door and vanished into the gloom.

Sue had a cursory look in the front room. It had a wonderful view of the sea.

On the floor by the armchair in the bay window was a Friday newspaper open at a page with a large picture of a woman in a leather flying helmet smiling with her mouth closed.

The room was cold and she shivered.

Upstairs she found an unmade bed in the front bedroom and the same in the back. There were some clothes, not many, in the wardrobe in the front and very little else apart from toothpaste and other stuff in the bathroom.

Where had the neighbour gone?

She paused.

What was that sound? It was like a voice. A voice coming from downstairs.

She descended the stairs slowly and as quietly as possible.

It was indistinct, as if coming from a distance. Then it stopped.

She reached the bottom step and paused.

It had seemed to be coming from underneath the stairs.

She opened the brown cloakroom door and found the light switch. The bulb didn't come on.

"Hello?" she half whispered.

"Hello?" The voice half whispered back.

It was dark in the cloakroom. She thought she had passed a torch lying on the hall table. She came out and got it.

Turning it on she shone it into the tiny room to see another door to the right with the top right cut at an angle to accommodate the angle of the stairs.

It was dark brown too, set into dingy cream. She opened the spring-loaded catch and shone the torch in expecting to see the far wall.

Instead there was nothing but darkness.

The torchlight penetrated nothing. Its beam seemed to stop. She put out her hand and felt something cold and unyielding.

"Hello?"

Something seized her wrist and pulled her forwards into the darkness.

Chapter 13

Pushing past Alistair, Angharad pulled open the back door, ran down the damp steps to the end of the yard and looked over the wall both ways.

She came back very quietly, looking pale. "I don't know, cariad," she said, coming back into the kitchen.

"You see? There's nobody there, is there?"

"No."

"What does it look like?" He said pointing to the mark on the window.

She took her time looking at it carefully. "Looks like the mark of a football to me. Now who would do such a silly thing?"

"So where's the football then?"

"I don't know. I haven't looked. It's dark down there between the steps and the garage."

"Well, have a look!"

Angharad looked at him angrily. "Don't go bossing me about, mister!"

"I'm sorry."

"Come on, we'll go back to mine and have a look in the morning. Now mind yourself down the steps, they're a bit slippery."

He grasped both rails coming down and stood at the bottom as she pulled the door closed and locked it.

"Huh! Forgotten the case!" She said suddenly and had to open up and retrieve it.

They made their way out of the yard and back to her house.

Jeff was there with the fish and chips in the kitchen. Suddenly Alistair felt very hungry.

"Thought you weren't coming," Jeff said his mouth full.

Angharad frowned, "You haven't scoffed it all, have you?"

"Would I ever!"

"You might have put it in the warm oven. Men! I dunno! You go and sit in the front, Alistair, while I put the kettle on. I think we both need a brew."

"Saw something, din't you?" Jeff said, indistinctly, his mouth full of chips.

"That's none of your business, is it?" his sister said.

"I wouldn't go messing with them, if I was you."

Angharad said nothing and busied herself with the tea, putting the remaining fish and chips in the oven and turning the heat up a bit.

Alistair sat in the comfortable front room. A crescent moon hung over the cliff with the war memorial on. Everything was so normal. So quiet. It was hard to believe that anything had really happened only inches away through that wall. If there was something why hadn't it seeped through just inches of brick?

By the time they'd finished their meal it was getting late. Jeff had gone to bed. Every time he had opened his mouth to say anything Angharad glared at him so he said nothing but affected to read the paper, though it was obvious he was keeping both eye and ear on his sister.

"Can I wash up?" Alistair asked.

"Oh. All right. I'll just make up the spare bed."

In the kitchen he stared out of the window into the back lane. A small orange street lamp attached to a telegraph pole shone wanly on the wet lane. Nothing could be seen outside its pool of light.

Angharad came back into the kitchen.

"Come on then, let's get you to bed. It'll all seem different in the morning. We'll look for that football, okay?" She gestured him through the door.

Alistair felt very tired." Okay. And thank you."

*****

Alistair dreamt. Of that woman with snakes gliding up her back – only this time they were real snakes. In unison they turned their heads and hissed at him.

"Breakfast!"

"Wha'?" He surfaced from sleep as Angharad opened the curtains. The bright sun flooded in. He closed his eyes tightly. "Can you close them please?" he said weakly.

He heard the curtain rings grate along the runners.

"Okay, now?"

"Thanks."

"Porridge is on the go. You better come quick or Jeff will have eaten it all!"

He threw on his clothes and gingerly made his way down unfamiliar stairs to the sound and smell of bacon frying.

"Ah, there you are!" She put a large bowl of porridge in front of him. "Put a good lining on your stomach. Heaven knows when you last had a proper meal. Thin as a lath you are!"

Porridge was not exactly his favourite, but he got it down somehow.

"How do you like your eggs? Well done or runny?"

"No, really – I …"

"Growing lad like you needs a good breakfast – and stop putting so much marmalade on your toast – you'll bankrupt me you will!!" she said to Jeff, who winced.

"There!" She put a huge plate of bacon, eggs and fried slice in front of him.

Heart-attack city, he thought. But it was good.

"Local eggs, local bacon – can't beat it!" she said sitting down.

After breakfast she washed up speedily. "Ready to face the dragon?"

Jeff looked up from studying his fingernails. "You shouldn't joke about such things."

Angharad said nothing, but gave him a thunderous look.

Alistair breathed in. "Okay."

The sun was out on the back of the house and it looked extremely unthreatening – almost as if it were saying "Who, me?"

The 'well' at the back of the house was bathed in sunshine shining directly into it. The outside lavatory door to his left faced the side of the steps up to the kitchen. It was open.

"They've been in there again smooching or worse," she said. "You'd better put a padlock on it."

She went in and came out holding a white football with black markings slightly the worse for wear. "There's your culprit, isn't it? Must of bounced in there after hitting the window. Kids, eh?"

He took the ball gingerly as if it might bite. He was not convinced.

"Why so solemn, then? Mystery solved!" she beamed.

He handed the ball back to her. "Where's the lacing?"

"What do you mean?"

"This is a modern plastic ball. There's the valve hole for blowing it up. Old leather balls had a rubber inside with a tube for blowing it up by mouth which was then laced back into the ball. That was the imprint I saw the first time and last night."

"All I saw was a smudgy roundy thing. Don't you think you were seeing what you wanted to see?"

He rubbed his hand over his forehead, "Oh, I don't know."

"Come on, let's get back. I'll put a note in the corner shop window later, see if anybody turns up claiming it."

Back in her house she put the ball down on the kitchen table. Jeff wandered in. He took one look at it.

"That's not it."

Angharad sighed. "How would you know?"

"Doesn't feel right."

Alistair looked at Angharad and then at Jeff and said tightly, "I think I'd better be making a move. She said I was to stay at The Artemis. And I've trespassed on your kindness too much already."

Jeff narrowed his eyes "Who's *she*?"

"The local nutter," Angharad said.

"Oh. You mean Stephanie. The wise woman."

Angharad snorted." Wise woman my a…"

"She knows not to go blundering into things."

Angharad reared up. "And I do, I suppose?"

Alistair didn't want to share this row. It was nothing to do with him.

"Look, I'd better go. Thanks for everything."

Angharad looked round and smiled "Well you know where to come. You'll always find a welcome here."

"Thanks, sorry and all that."

He pulled open the kitchen door and went slowly down the back steps leaving an ominous silence behind him.

Chapter 14

"That's not the right ball," Jeff said again. "I know it."

"Oh, for God's sake! What would you know about it?"

"It's too modern. Whatsha let him go for? Heaven knows what he's letting himself in for. Them Dysons is odd at the best of times."

"I know you don't get on with Jim Dyson – but you oughta put that behind you."

Jeff leaned back against the door jamb. "Still if Stephanie says he should stay there …"

Angharad stood up. "Enough of your nonsense! I'm going to put a card in the window of the corner shop right now – see who claims it."

"Bet no one will. They won't want to be thought trespassing. You can pick up a new one cheap just over the road."

"Well, we'll see."

"Dead waste of 50p if you ask me."

Angharad's mouth twitched, but she said nothing, leaving the room and coming back with a polaroid instant picture camera.

After she taken a picture of the ball and waved the print in the air for a few seconds until the image appeared she opened the kitchen door and descended the steps.

The wind was blowing hard but it wasn't far to the corner shop where she got a form and filled it in.

"What's all that about?" the middle-aged redhead from the post office extension at the other end of the main counter said, leaning over Angharad's shoulder.

"Found it in Jones's back yard this morning."

"What were you doing in there then?" she asked, a half smile on her lips. "You interested in him then?"

"No. Should I be?"

"Go on!" She nudged Angharad in the side. "Nice looking bloke, own house, right next to yours – what's not to like?"

"Gwen, stop it! Always matchmaking you are. I'm quite happy as I am thank you!"

"Go orn!" She smiled and turned away, going back to her end of the counter and lifting the flap. "Can't wait to get a new hat!"

Several heads turned in the queue that was building up at the general counter and Angharad could feel her face burn.

She handed over her 50p to Owen on the other side of the counter who pulled at his greying moustache and mouthed the words on the form. "Right you are, then! I'll put a card in this afternoon. Don't think anyone's going to own up though."

*****

Alistair walked dejectedly up the village.

It was still early in the day – what was he going to do? Go back to The Artemis and frowst in his room, bored to tears all day, looking out on a grey rolling sea? Suppose he was seen, face beside the drawn back grubby net curtains? *'Bugger!'* he thought.

He looked up at the sky and then down at his feet – and came to a decision. 'Tintagel' the archaeologist had said. Open invitation he said. Time to take him up on it – whether he meant it or not.

It was further than he thought. He'd only seen the back vaguely from the beach and had no means of telling how far it was in reference to the street.

He went past a road on his right stretching into the distance between hedges and reed beds, past quite a few houses – one a double fronted with windows of frosted glass halfway up –

There it was. The house with steps straight off the road opposite a cafe. Dark blue, not pink as it was on the seaside. He mounted the steps and looked for a bell. Finding none he rapped sharply with the knocker above the letterbox.

Nothing happened for a bit and he was about to raise it again when a shadow crossed the light behind the frosted glass strips in the door and it was pulled open with an effort.

The man's face changed from a scowl to a half smile.

"Oh, hello! It's that desecrater of sunken forests!" The voice was light and jokey.

"Yes. That's me. Got a minute?"

"Sure. Come away in. You'll have to forgive the mess. Bachelor's privilege."

Alistair stepped into a scratched brown panelled corridor and followed Archie towards the back of the house, briefly catching sight of an untidy kitchen through a half open door to his right.

The room smelled musty and was full of rather broken down grubby-looking brown furniture with boxes everywhere. French windows looked out onto a conservatory stacked with more boxes and tools of various kinds leaning at crazy angles. The sea and the sky were beyond.

"Do sit down. Tea? Don't get many visitors."

"But I thought you said …"

"Sugar?"

"No, thanks."

"Back in a tick."

Alistair sat down gingerly in an armchair whose seat was definitely concave and felt as uncomfortable as it looked.

The wallpaper was a dingy patterned brown and cream and in places curling away from the joints.

But as he looked round he saw it. A massive cranium with antlers looming over at him from the opposite wall. It gave him the willies.

Archie came bustling in with two mugs and some biscuits on a tray.

"Ah, you've discovered my pride and joy!" he said, setting the tray down on a low table strewn with magazines.

"Not real of course. Original's in the museum in Traethmor. Only acrylic I'm afraid. But he's magnificent isn't he?" He sat down, coughing as a cloud of dust ascended.

"Help yourself! Yes, it's the cranium and antlers of a red deer stag found in the sand at the far end of Aberceldy by a couple of dog walkers. It died somewhere between 12,000 and 24,000 B.C. during the winter and the following spring. It would have been roaming the beech forest close to the shore. Might have been hunted down – who knows? Fascinating!" He clapped his hands together and rubbed them.

"Well, drink up! What can I do you for?"

"Nothing, really. You said I might drop by."

"So I did! So I did!"

"So what sort of things have you found round here?"

"Fascinating cliffs you know. Shrouded in myth. The Cave of the White Lady, the water monster Barfog and so on. Slates and greywacke."

"Greywacke?"

"Compressed mudstones. Occasional fossil of some unfortunate animal. Let me show you some."

He got up and wandered around the room haphazardly inspecting various boxes. "Now where did I put them? Aha! Yes.

Here we are!" He picked up a box and dropped it on the table where it nearly fell off as the slithering magazines moved. "Here! Take a look at that!"

Alistair took a flattish slate with the imprint of a curled spiral creature.

"Ammonite. A creature of warm Devonian seas. They grew to a huge size – no natural predators then you see – this one is only a baby! And how about this!" He snatched back the ammonite and thrust another something at him. "Trilobite! Magnificent creature!"

To Alistair it looked like a giant armoured slug.

"What did they do?"

"Wandered about bottom feeding or sucking in smaller lifeforms. But we do know that trilobites were not predatory – no mandibles you see. Intestines and stuff don't survive fossilisation. Mind you I do have one or two theories –"

There was a sharp series of knocks on the front door.

"Wonder who that can be?" said Archie getting to his feet and wandering out of the room.

'*Don't get many visitors*,' Alistair thought. '*I wonder –*'

He heard the door pulled open, a murmur of voices and the door pushed closed again. Then silence. Archie came back in followed by a tall gaunt faced man whose pin sharp black eyes fixed on Alistair with an unpleasant stare.

"Sorry to interrupt our chat, Alistair. Something's come up. So …"

Alistair got up and stretched out his hand to the man "Pleased to meet you, Mr – er –?" The other man didn't move, but went on pinning him with his eyes.

"Right. Well, thanks for the tea …"

"Sorry to cut it short. See you again I hope, Alistair?" said Archie ushering him out and down the corridor to the door. He pulled it open with difficulty. "Must get this door seen to – damp, you know."

Alistair looked out. Rain had just started bouncing on the road. Terrific.

He descended the steps as the door closed behind him and ran across the road looking for that cafe he had spotted. Thankfully it was open.

Wrenching open the door he found himself in a narrow room with Formica topped tables down both sides underneath black-and-white photographs on the wall of what could be the village. He sat down at one on his left and then wondered what to do next. There was no one else in here. He picked up a stained dark red plastic covered menu and opened it.

A door to his right squeaked open and a large woman in a blue nylon overall with short sleeves and a stained apron over the top came in.

"What can I get you?"

Well, he'd better have something. Can't just say I've only come in to keep out of the rain.

"Wait a minute," she said suddenly, "You're him, aren't you?"

"Beg pardon?"

"She was in enquiring about you. You fit her description. You're the one who's bought Jones's house past the lifeboat station near the cliff aren't you?"

"Why, yes. But what did she look like?"

"About so high, frizzy and unruly dark hair, black rimmed square glasses …"

"You've seen Sue?"

"Oh, yes. Quite a chat we had."

"When was this?"

"Oooh. Saturday I think it was now."

Two days ago or was it three? He was confused as to time.

"Have you seen her since?"

"No. Can't say as I have."

"This is important. Where was she going?"

"She was staying at the Dysons – The Diana you know – she may have said she was going to your house. Yes, I am almost sure …"

"Thanks," he said, getting up.

"You're not staying ? "

"No. Can't. She's in danger. I just know it. The house …"

"Oh, yes. We all know about the house."

He ran to the door and yanked it open, ran through the rain.

Sue! Sue! I'm coming love …

Soaked to the skin he arrived at the house. The front door was locked. Of course! He didn't have any keys. Got to go round to Angharad's.

He went down the passage at the side of the house. Side door wouldn't open. Must be bolted on the other side. Shit! Why is everything so bloody difficult?

He ran up the road towards the cliff searching for a passageway to the back lane. There was one! A narrow one between a house and a low white cottage – its door and windows facing blankly onto the path.

Out into the back lane and round to Angharad's. Up the steps. Bang on the door. Come on! Come on!

The door was pulled open and there was Jeff standing there.

"She's not in!"

"Who isn't?"

"Who are you looking for?"

"The girl you met in the chip shop cafe."

"Ah. Angharad let her into your house."

"Yes. And?"

"She ain't been seen since."

"You got the key?"

"I don' know where she keeps it."

Before he knew what he was doing Alistair had grabbed him by his shabby grey jumper and was shaking him.

"Where's the bloody key?"

"All right, all right, Duw!" He shook himself free. "Sit down, man, sit down."

"What?"

"Do you really want to get into this?"

"What do you mean?"

"Just sit down will you?" The man was getting testy.

"Why are you suddenly talking like this?"

"I'm just as sane as you. It's an act."

Alistair was stunned. "What?"

"Will you please stop saying *what* all the time? Just sit down!"

Alistair sat down unsteadily.

"No, not there. Other end of the table, so you're hidden by the curtain. Anybody comes in or past it looks like I'm talking to myself. Everybody thinks I'm potty anyway."

Alistair sat down gingerly behind the curtain.

"Right. Ready?"

Alistair nodded.

"I pretend to be an idiot so they'll leave me alone."

"Who?" He was finding it difficult to take all this in.

"The villagers. Not all of them – but a fair number. I think they've released something or opened a portal to somewhere and now they're scared. They don't know what to do."

Then something clicked in Alistair's head. All the odd little things people have been saying.

Alistair stared at Jeff. "The woman in the chip shop told me 'We know about that house'."

"Well, they think they do. The only one who has any idea is the white witch."

"The white witch? "

"Stephanie Chambers!"

Alistair half smiled. "But even your own sister thinks you're a bit touched!"

"Grief affects different people in different ways. When my wife died I did go off the rails. Started seeing and hearing things that weren't there. But eventually I came to terms with it. Trouble was some things were still there when I got better."

"Like what?"

"You know the stair rails in your house? Parts of the house are designed specifically to generate an aura – Jones was an antiquary – he dug into all sorts of odd books in the National Library – well it's only up the road. Went down to London to the British Library and spent hours there. Said he'd cracked the Voynich Manuscript."

"I've heard of it vaguely. Isn't it something to do with Roger Bacon, the mystic in the 13th century?"

"Got it. The script is in a totally unknown form – possibly symbols. But it's got nothing to do with Bacon. Radiocarbon dating shows it to be early 15th century." Jeff leaned back and breathed out.

"So what I'm saying is you re-enter that house at your peril. It's onto you."

He got up and went over to the kettle and was in the act of filling it when the door squeaked open.

Angharad looked grave she came in and then brightened up as soon as she saw Alistair.

"Just makin' a cup o' tea. Lad came in soaked. Lookin' for that girl what you showed roun' next door." The body language, simple expression and speech patterns were back. The man was a chameleon.

Angharad glared at him. Then she smiled. "She went away after I'd shown her you weren't there."

Alistair heard Jeff cough as he plugged in the kettle.

"Well, this is nice!" Angharad said. She leaned forward and touched Alistair's sleeve. "You are damp. I don't know- turning up muddy and now wet! What are we going to do with you, cariad?"

"Oh, I'll dry out in a bit."

"Can't have you catching cold. I'll go and get those clothes you were wearing before like."

"No, it's okay –"

But she had already gone out of the door.

Jeff put a mug of tea in front of him and tapped the side of his nose. "Not a word now," he whispered.

She came back with the clothes. "You can change in the front room if you like."

"Thanks, I will." He gathered them up and went across the hall.

As soon as he crossed the threshold his 'Friendship' ring began to tingle and then burn. Sue was in danger. He knew it. And somehow he also knew she was not far away. Maybe next door. No time to change his clothes. But he would need them. There was a supermarket bag lying on the settee. He crammed them in and ran to the front door. Locked.

He ran into the kitchen. Two faces turned towards him, amazement on their faces.

"Sorry, gotta go!"

"But your tea!" Angharad stood in front of the back door, blocking his exit.

He caught sight of Jeff out of the corner of his eye motioning him to sit down.

He sat.

"A slice of cake?" Angharad asked.

"No, just the tea will be fine."

"So where are you going all of a sudden?" Angharad hadn't moved from the door.

"Just remembered something I had to do, that's all."

"Still in your damp clothes?"

"I'll live. Look, I've got the dry ones here – I'll be all right." He drank down the scalding tea. "Now I really must be going."

He got up and walked towards Angharad. He was going to force his way past if need be.

For a moment she looked as if she wasn't going to let him pass – but then smiled and moved aside. He ran down the steps, wondering what to do.

He couldn't get into the house – but maybe if he went to have a look at it – maybe there would be a light on or something.

He went round into the yard. No sign of life.

He unbolted the side door into the passage and went up it round to the front.

Suddenly the ring gave him the most terrible pull to his right. He looked up the road. There she was!

Chapter 15

The hand let go of Sue's wrist.

"Hello? Where are you?" Her voice didn't echo or sound loud but muffled, as if she was talking into a soundproof room.

She turned round, but there was no sign of the door behind her. Just thick darkness. All around.

"Hello?" Her voice wavered. She was beginning to feel really frightened. Oh, why, why did she go sticking her nose into things?

A pool of pearly light appeared on what must be a floor some distance away, broadening out into an ellipse, but not growing any brighter.

Trying to test the ground with first one foot then the other, she moved carefully forward, afraid that at any moment she would reach an edge in the dark and tip, flailing, into the void.

The temperature all round her was neither cold or warm, but a sort of ... nothing.

Hardly daring to breathe she arrived at the pool of light and, trembling all over, stepped into it.

Nothing happened.

She looked round her. The light didn't seem to come from anywhere, but just was there encasing her. She put her hand out and then her arm through the light. They disappeared into the dimness in which she could just make them out.

"Hello? Can you hear me?"

Nothing.

Then a very slight whispering, a breathing in her ear, on the edge of hearing. She could be imagining it.

Grey cloaked figures gathered all round her, their faces in shadow, their hands enfolded in their robes.

"Please speak to me! You're frightening me!"

One tall figure stepped forward. The sleeves of its robes fell back showing slim hands as it swept back its hood. A boyish, but unmistakably female, face with red curly hair cut short in a fringe at her forehead. Her dark green eyes fixed on Sue. Her lips parted showing a gap in her top set of teeth.

"Please don't be afraid. I am Amelia Earhart. I have come … We have come … to give you a message … to give you a message for The Lamplighter."

Sue felt she was on the edge of a scream. "But you're dead …" Her voice came out as no more than a whisper.

"Not dead, but waiting here in the Bardo. All of us." She gestured round her and Sue turned to find she was surrounded by similarly robed figures, some with their hoods drawn back, some unmistakably revealing they were wearing football shirts or airman's helmets or military uniforms underneath their cloaks.

"What … What is your message?" Sue faltered.

There were whispers all round her, rising to a crescendo. Then Amelia Earhart spoke, "Tell him … Tell him … Remember … Remember January the eleventh."

The light went out.

Sue put out her right hand and hit something hard with the ends of her fingers.

What was going on?

Somehow she realised she had her eyes shut and opened them.

She was lying on the dusty floor with the light coming from behind her. She raised her head. To her right and left was darkness.

She sat up feeling dizzy and found that she had been lying full length in the cloakroom with the door open to the tiny room under the stairs.

Had she imagined it all? But it had been so real ...

She grabbed the edge of the doorway and painfully heaved herself upright.

All was silence.

She staggered out into the hall, into the kitchen. Looking out into the yard there was no one about. She tried the back door.

Locked.

That bitch has locked me in.

She sat down at the kitchen table and tried to think. Why had that woman relented and let her into the house, only to lock her in? She touched the back of her head. It felt tender. Had she been hit? Or was it just left over from when she'd fallen down the entry?

But why had she locked her in? Did she know something? Did she intend her never to come out, but be lost forever in darkness – or had she passed out and imagined the whole thing?

She got herself some water in a mug from the draining board. At least he had been here. The mug was clean. It wasn't dusty. It had been washed recently. But where was he?

Somebody passed by in the lane. She banged on the window and shouted even though it hurt her head. But they just walked on by. Silently.

Got to get out. Got to find him. Tell him about his awful neighbour.

The front door was locked.

She went into the front room.

There on the floor by an armchair with its back to the window was the newspaper open at the page which read 'Amelia Earhart: New evidence found'.

That was it. She remembered seeing it before. She had dreamt the whole thing. Her subconscious had remembered it and constructed everything.

But then who had pulled her into the dark? It must have been someone? But why? Why?

She was going to have it out with that bitch. But first she had to get out.

She looked at the windows. Sash windows. How old-fashioned! She examined the lock.

Simple.

Unscrew the ring thing on the little arm that held it against the bracket on the bottom of the upper window, swing it round and – bingo!

She pulled up the bottom window and carefully eased herself out onto the front yard.

She shivered in the cold wind slicing across the front. Shaking from the effort and from her escape from the airless house she sat down on the wall next to the pillar to her right next to the gate entrance to the road. Should she go round and face the bitch? No. In her present state that would not be a good idea.

Maybe she should go back to The Artemis? But it was a long way.

She was at a loss as to what she should do.

Chapter 16

She couldn't sit here all day.

Sue dragged herself up by clutching onto the pillar and set off up the village feeling sick.

But she'd only got about a hundred yards or so when she was overcome with tiredness and shaking in her legs.

Not far ahead she saw a black-and-white lean-to on the side of a house. The Limit Cafe. *'Well, I've certainly reached my limit,'* she thought grimly.

She sagged onto a chipped blue painted wooden chair and cradled her head in her hands on the scratched table. Watery sunshine caressed her hair.

She heard a door open and footsteps. With a rattle a teacup and saucer were put down in front of her.

She opened her eyes and saw a light green old-fashioned cup and saucer inches from her nose.

"Thought you could do with this. Are you all right, Cariad?"

It was a soft Welsh female voice. She looked up.

A woman in a flowered pinny over a pink cardigan looked at her out of a lined face and kind eyes.

"Can I sit with you?"

Sue nodded. She didn't feel like doing anything else.

"Want to tell me about it?"

Sue shook her head and then thought, '*What the hell.*'

"Just escaped from a house."

"Just escaped from a house! Duw," the woman stretched out a hand and patted Sue's upper arm. "What a terrible thing! Emlyn! Emlyn! Come out here at once! This poor girl's had a terrible shock!"

"No, it's all right. I don't want to make a fuss!" Sue said, jerking up her head, realising what she had done.

"No fuss, cariad. Drink your tea and tell us about it."

"No, really, it's all right." She took a sip of tea and then a big gulp. That was good.

"Emlyn, get her another one!"

A man emerged from the cafe wiping his hands on a cloth. "Right away."

The woman patted Sue on her hand.

"So what happened?"

"I was looking for a friend and I went to his house. Someone let me in and then they locked the door!"

"Dew! Who would do such a thing? Which house was that then?"

Sue couldn't help herself. "The one along the front, past the lifeboat station. Faded green paint."

A shadow passed over the woman's face and her mouth suddenly hardened. "Jones's place."

"You know it?"

"Everyone knows Jones's place. Bad place. Bad news for anyone who bought it."

A shadow fell across her.

"Thank God I've found you!"

Sue half turned – and there he was.

Alistair.

He bent down and pulled her to him.

She hugged him until she thought her arms would break.

And began to cry, slowly at first and then with great racking sobs.

*****

Angharad's face was white with fury.
"What did you tell him?"
Jeff backed up against the sink unit.
"I don' know what you're talking about, woman!"
Angharad advanced on him, prodding him in the chest with a horny forefinger. "Oh, yes, you, do. You think I don't know this is all an act! It may have been true once but – what did you tell him? Why did he take off like that? Where's he gone?
"How should I know?"
"You told him – didn't you – that I took her to the house!"
"Will you stop goin' on at me!"
"And you saw what he'd got round his neck when he took his top off to put on Idris's old tracksuit top. That thing round his neck. That's a protective charm, that is – must've been given to him by that madwoman! Wait 'til I see her – interfering old hag!"
Jeff stayed silent. As long as Alistair believed in that charm he should be okay, he thought. He thought he knew why Alistair had taken off – but he wasn't going to tell his sister.

*****

Archie looked down at the note the man had brought him and then up from his seat on the settee.
"Well, we know where he's been last night and where he's staying. But something is shielding him. And we know where he got that don't we? You'd better go and deal with her."
The man with the piercing eyes loomed over him.
"You out of your mind? It's more than my life's worth to tangle with her!"
"I suppose you want me to do it?"

"You are head of our order."

Archie tossed the note aside angrily. "All right! If you want a job doing properly do it yourself! You'd better go and pick them up."

"What, both of them?"

"Well, we can't afford any loose cannons can we? That girl's been poking her nose in too much already. Angharad says she doesn't show any sign of going back to Birmingham. Get your uniform on. Got diesel in the tank?"

"Sure. I know my job."

"Right. Get to it."

Chapter 17

Sue rubbed her eyes with the heel of her hand. "Sorry to be such a prat!"

Alistair sat down opposite her, the owners having retreated to the door of the cafe. He didn't quite know what she meant by that, but anyway … "I knew you were in Aberceldy. Saw your signature in the visitors' book at The Artemis. Some really strange things have been going on round here –"

"You're telling me!"

"You mean –"

"I think she ought to go to bed," said the woman coming forward. "Where are you staying, Cariad?"

"The Artemis."

"Orrh, that's a long walk. Don't worry, bus'll be along in a minute. Here it comes now, see?"

A small single decker could be seen coming down the village towards them.

"If you get on it now it'll go along the front, up the hill, turn round by the council houses and then it'll come back down past here and through the village. Just ask the driver to put you off."

Alistair helped her up, but the moment she turned to face the bus, he felt her stiffen. The doors banged open.

"Something's not right," she said in a low voice.

The driver turned slightly towards them – and then Alistair knew. It was the man with the eyes at Archie's house.

Alistair raised his voice – "It's all right, we'll wait for you to come back past. She needs to rest a bit more."

The man nodded and drove on.

He whispered in her ear. "Take it nice and slowly. Don't look left or right."

She nodded.

"Thanks for looking after – oh – and thanks for the tea."

"But it won't be a minute." The woman seemed agitated. She blocked their path.

"No, we're fine," he said, sidestepping her and pulling Sue after him, "She just needs air and maybe a little walk."

He felt Sue stumble and held her up. He looked round at her. Her face was pale and sweating.

How long would it take the bus to turn round he didn't know, but at least they would get a head start. The beginnings of a plan began to form in the back of his mind

He tried to get her to move faster, but she couldn't manage it.

In the distance behind them he could hear a diesel engine straining and then the shriek of air brakes and a horn. Then it was getting closer, closer. He could somehow feel the heat from it.

Then it was right alongside them, keeping pace.

He felt like stopping and shouting at it – "Bugger off will you!" But there were few people about – and perhaps they were all in league with the driver? A cold shudder ran down his back.

They passed the road on the left that disappeared into the distance between reed beds

Then just on the corner – salvation! At least he hoped so. The doctors' surgery. He realised he'd seen it when looking for Archie – the double fronted house with frosted glass windows. He could see the brass plaque quite plainly now – Dr W. C. and Dr R. Davies.

"In here," he said, wrenching the door open.

Inside they were in a corridor. To his left was a dark red door with more frosted glass in it and a plaque below reading 'Reception'.

He pushed it open and a surprised receptionist looked up from her desk, her thick glasses catching the light.

"Doctor's not in 'till five. It's only 4.30 now," she said in a Midlands accent. "I should've locked the door."

"This is an emergency! She's hit her head!"

The receptionist peered at Sue. "You do look pale, love. Come in and sit down," she said, her face softening. "Doctor's not here yet. Can I get you a glass of water?"

"Thanks, that would be great," he said.

As soon as she gone out he turned to Sue. "We better have a cover story."

Sue nodded and squeezed his hand. "I did hit my head on a low door earlier – I think … it's all a bit confused."

"Okay. We'll go with that."

He heard the street door open and male voices murmuring – and the sound of a diesel engine idling. He looked round and could just see the blurred outline of the bus through the frosted glass. They – whoever they were – weren't going to give up easily.

The receptionist came back in with a glass of water. "Doctor's here. Shouldn't be long now." She handed the glass to Sue. "Where you from, love?"

Sue took a sip of the water. "Birmingham."

"Here on holiday?"

"Yes."

The woman looked at her narrowly, "Bit out of season?"

"I came to visit my friend here."

"Arh. Could I have a few details – date of birth?"

While all this was going on Alistair tried to think what to do when they'd seen the doctor and had to come out. If there was a back door onto a car park …

"Right. I'll just take this temporary visitors card through to the doctor. Won't be long." The door closed behind her.

Alistair squeezed her hand. "How are you feeling?"

"A bit better," she said, taking another sip. "But that bloody bus is still out there. What are we going to do?"

"I'm just hoping there's a back door onto the car park. I'll pretend I've got a car."

"Always assuming there is a car park."

They heard the street door open again and a loud female voice shout – "Get that thing out of here! I've told you before. This space is reserved for doctors on call. Go on! Park it up the road, why don't you – better still go home!"

She came back in muttering.

"Is there a problem?" Alistair asked pleasantly.

"It's that blasted Ben and his old bus. If I've told him once –"

She was interrupted as a buzzer sounded and one of the glass boxes on the wall lit up "Dr C. N. W. Davies."

"You can go in now. Second door on your left."

"Thank you."

He made a great show of helping Sue to her feet and they went out. In the dim corridor He knocked on the door marked 'Dr Cynwy Davies'.

"Come."

Inside was a sunny functional room. He could see through the open venetian blind that there was a car park. That was a relief. Beyond to the right was the road lined with hedges.

Someone clearing their throat brought him back into the room. Behind a desk was a white-haired man with an open intelligent pink face, a stethoscope round his neck. His desk was empty except for a wooden filing tray, a blotting pad and an old, green, dial telephone.

"Would you take a seat please?"

They sat.

"And what can I do for you today, Miss Masters?"

"She's banged her head."

"I'm sure Miss Masters can answer for herself Mr – er?"

"Powell."

"Ah, yes, Jones's place. So?"

Sue spoke slowly and quietly. "I was looking under the stairs – there's a door off the cloakroom and the lintel must have been low and the next thing I knew I was laid out on the floor."

"I see."

"I heard this thud and came out of the sitting room and there she was." Alistair said.

"I see. Well, we'd better have a look."

The doctor took some disposable gloves out of a drawer in his desk and put them on.

"Would you like to get on the bed and I'll draw the screens?"

Sue looked scared and grabbed Alistair's hand. "No, it's all right thank you."

The Doctor got up, came round the desk and carefully parted Sue's hair.

"Raise your right arm above shoulder height."

She obeyed and winced.

The Doctor looked at her piercingly. "That was some fall wasn't it?"

"Yes."

"Not today though. Undo your blouse for me would you? I want to listen to your heart."

Sue shivered as the end of the stethoscope was applied to her.

"Sorry. Medicine hasn't come up with a warm one yet. Right. Lean forward please." She felt it pressed over different parts of her back. Then heard a click as the doctor replaced it round his neck.

Dr Davies sat down carefully behind his desk. He looked at her for a few moments.

"What are you afraid of?"

This took Sue by such surprise that she gasped. Could she trust him? Suppose he was in league with – who?

"I know – you're worried in case I'm in league with some of the villagers."

Could he read her mind? She passed her hand over her brow and found it was sweating.

"Well, put your mind at rest – I'm not. Though I would be very useful to them, being at the hub of the community. It would not surprise you that manifold confidences pass through this consulting room." He paused. "My receptionist told me that Ben Waller was sitting outside here in his bus. So … What's been going on?"

Sue looked at Alistair, who nodded.

"I came down from Birmingham to look for Alistair. I went next door to his house to ask his neighbour if she'd seen him and she was most unpleasant. So I left and went to have one last look at the house and she came round with the key. I couldn't understand what she was up to. She let me in and I looked all over the house to see if he'd been in recently and when I came downstairs I heard this voice coming from the cloakroom. I took a torch from the hall table and discovered another room leading off it under the stairs. The next thing I was flat out on the floor and the house had been locked up."

"You've left something out."

For a second time she was afraid he was reading her mind.

"I had this strange vision of being surrounded by people in the dark – I was standing in a pool of light – and one of them … was Amelia Earhart."

She heard Alistair give a sharp intake of breath.

"I don't know if it was a dream or what."

"So, Mr Powell, you've seen her too?"

Alistair was afraid. What was happening?

The doctor raised an eyebrow.

"Yes."

The doctor's lips compressed and then relaxed. "I'm not going to say 'don't worry'. There's a lot going on in the village that I don't understand. There are some crackpot organisations but unfortunately they may have stumbled on something they don't understand – and neither do I."

Sue leaned forward. "But what should we do?"

"The immediate problem is to get you away from Mr Waller. Did you come by car, Mr Powell?"

"No. I found Sue sitting outside The Limit cafe. This bus turned up and I thought it was okay until I saw the man driving it. I'd seen him at Mr Dugdale's and took an instant dislike to him. Sue felt there was something wrong too so we walked here followed by that wretched bus."

"These are deep matters, Mr Powell. I'll give you my telephone number. Don't hesitate to ring me day or night. I'll have a word with a friend of mine –"

Alistair put his hand to his chin. "That wouldn't be Stephanie Chambers would it?"

The Doctor smiled "Ah, so you've met our Stephanie? I trust she's been keeping an eye on you?"

"I hope so."

"Anyway. The back door leads out to the car park onto the road down to the river. But where will you go then?"

"We're staying at The Artemis – independently of course."

The doctor smiled again. "Of course. Then I suggest you make your way there via various back lanes, keeping out of sight of the High Street. The Dysons aren't part of any organisation as far as I know – so you should be okay for a bit. As to you, Miss Masters, your head wound has been expertly sewn up – how did you fall?"

"I fell down a step in the entry between Alistair's house and next door in the dark"

"And how are you feeling now?"

"I've had a couple of days in hospital, so I'm not too bad."

"Well, I suggest you go to bed for the rest of the day. Take some paracetamol if you're in pain – but nothing else at the moment. Here's my telephone number."

"Do you have a mobile?" asked Sue.

"What's one of those?"

There was a sound of raised voices in the corridor.

"I fear Mr Waller thinks the birds have flown. Don't worry. Megan will take care of him. We'll just wait a minute."

A door slammed.

"Right. You'd better lose yourselves quickly." He hustled them out into the corridor and unlocked the back door. "Good luck!"

Sue turned to him. "Thank you, doctor."

"Don't mention it, young lady."

They were out in the car park. To their right was the exit onto the side road. But emerging onto it there didn't seem to be any cover. Sheds, a substation, some low bungalows – and then over the railway line ditches both sides of the road full of reeds.

Alistair looked to left and right. "We'll just have to hope for the best."

They got over the railway line and into the narrow lane. The same horses that Alistair had seen before were quietly grazing. Then the one that had 'spoken' to Alistair raised its head and looked up the lane.

At the same moment he heard the sound of an engine and, looking round, he saw the bus squeezing round the bend, its gears grating.

"Run!" he shouted.

"I can't!"

The horse neighed and Alistair looked towards it. It shook its head and fixed an eye on him. It knew.

Then, without a moment's hesitation the horse turned, ran in a tight circle, came back at a gallop and leapt over the hedge, clearing it easily. Landing on the road it turned its head towards Alistair, whinnied and then turned to face the bus. It came on.

From a standing start the horse galloped forward to within feet of the vehicle. The bus ground forward, but the horse did not give an inch.

Alistair pulled Sue to him, hugging her tightly, cold in the pit of his stomach.

The driver, looking white in the face, gunned the engine. In answer the horse reared up and brought its hooves down on the windscreen, shattering it into a myriad spider's webs.

The bus halted and the plainly terrified driver leapt from the cab and ran, screaming, up the lane towards the main road. The horse galloped after him.

Alistair stood, open mouthed. He grabbed Sue's hand and they, somehow, ran towards the river which ran between high banks at right angles to the lane.

Scrambling up the bank, across the path at the top and down the other side they hunkered down on a sort of ledge above the swift flowing water, breathing heavily.

"I – don't – believe – it!" Sue said between breaths.

Alistair didn't answer. He couldn't believe it either. But now he was sure – the horse had spoken to him earlier. What on earth was going on? And why didn't the doctor know what a mobile was?

Chapter 18

Archie Dugdale slapped the other man hard across the face. "Stop gibbering! I don't want to hear about magical horses! Are you out of your mind? What did you want to go and draw attention to yourself for? Now they'll recognise you – may even know who you are. What do you think you were doing, trailing them in your bus?"

"I only thought … we can't trace him normally, so I thought it would be a …" He dried up amid the other's stare.

"So now the doctor probably knows all about it?"

"But why would he talk to them about it?"

Archie sat down heavily. "Well, we've got to assume the worst. The only good thing is that now they're together we'll know where he is."

"If only we could get rid of her!"

Archie finally calmed down. "It's a dilemma I agree. She may strengthen him – which is what we don't want. But we will know where he is while she's with him."

"I suppose we could put her out of action for a bit. He won't want to sit by her bedside all day for days. You could knock up a potion."

"Knock up a potion! Sometimes I despair of you, Waller. It's not that easy and it takes days – you know that!"

"Only trying to help."

Archie sighed. Then he brightened up. "I wonder …"

*****

A cold wind barrelled down the river towards them and Sue shivered. "Why didn't the doctor know what a mobile phone was?"

Alistair looked up from contemplating the river. "I was thinking the same myself."

Sue got out her mobile from her bag and fiddled with the buttons. There was no signal. The battery was fully charged. "That's odd. It was working perfectly in the hospital when I spoke to John." Then something tweaked at the corner of her mind, but she couldn't think what it was. Something wasn't right. It looked sort of … different.

"Well, we are rather low down here," Alistair said.

"Perhaps that's it." But she wasn't convinced.

"I think we'd better make a move, don't you?"

She rose and brushed herself down. "I suppose so. You never know when he or someone else will come back. Better follow the river along. It'll keep us out of sight."

Coming to a bridge some distance along, Alistair scrambled up the bank to see how far they had got.

Coming back down he said, "There's a stile over the other side of the path that leads along the edge of a field of sheep and it looks like it comes out by the church. After that I can see the roof of the railway station."

"That's not far from The Artemis," she said

"We'd better make for that then."

Emerging by the church there was a tarmac lane, but not much cover. Low hedges stretched either side of it as far as the railway line. They walked up this as fast as possible, always aware of the windows of the tall houses in the distance, hoping no one was watching them.

They crossed the railway line, walked up the path to the station onto the platform and out through the empty waiting room into the road lined by Victorian villas. There was no one about.

Turning left at the end of the road they walked down to The Artemis and Sue inserted her key in the yale and went in.

The same stale smell of boiled cabbage greeted them, but as they were about to mount the stairs there was the sound of someone clearing their throat. Alistair whipped round and there was Stephanie Chambers standing in an open doorway to his left. She gestured with her head to follow her into the room.

Alistair went in to find Ms Chambers already sitting at a table for four in what was obviously the breakfast/dining room when the guesthouse was operating. The air was dusty and thin light filtered its way through the dirty net curtains. The scratched round tables were denuded of their cloths.

"I told you not to go back to the house," she said, looking angrily at Alistair. "Sit down at once."

Alistair sat. Sue remained standing. "I've already have had the unfortunate acquaintance of this woman, Alistair, so I'll just go up to my room."

Stephanie gave her a cursory glance. "As you wish."

Alistair sat staring at the ceiling until he heard the door shut.

"What were you thinking?" Stephanie said, icily.

Alistair lowered his gaze and counted to ten in his head. "How long do you suppose I could stay stuck in this place in only the clothes I stood up in, without even a toothbrush?"

A corner of the authoress's mouth twitched. "Now you've alerted the whole village. The moment you arrived at Angharad's house the bush telegraph swung into action. I suppose she's well-meaning, but she's a terrible gossip. And when you met this girl outside The Limit cafe the fat was truly in the fire. The Greys knew exactly where you were. One of them even tracked you up the village in his bus! It was only by the greatest good fortune that you escaped from the doctors'". She scraped her hands over her face. "I really don't know what to do for the best."

"Well, if you don't know ..."

"I fear she has let something out."

"What?"

"I don't know ... yet."

"You shouldn't have told her to go back to Birmingham. When she gets angry she just digs in ..."

"As I feared. You'd better go up to your room as well I think."

"Now wait a minute ..."

"These are deep matters far beyond you. Don't you want me to try and keep you safe?"

"Yes. But ..."

"Are you going?"

"All right. But you'd better come up with something or I am out of here!"

He got up, strode to the door and slammed it behind him.

Standing outside in the hall he looked up. Sue was hanging over the banisters. She raised her eyebrows. He made the motion of zipping his mouth and followed her up the stairs.

At the top, by unspoken consent, she followed him into his room and sat on the creaking bed.

Sue looked up at him. "I heard raised voices."

Alistair winced. "She started bossing me about. Said you should have gone back to Birmingham."

"Not while you're in danger."

"You're very sweet, but I don't want you to be hurt. She said something's got out – and even she doesn't know what to do about it."

The light was fading so he switched on the single, naked light bulb and sat next to her. She stretched out her hand and gave his a long squeeze.

"That woman is awful. I think she already looks upon you as her property."

"What woman?"

"The woman that lives next to your house."

Alistair stared at her, "What makes you say that?"

"I went round looking for you. She couldn't wait to get rid of me. Then she did something really weird."

"What?"

"She let me into your house."

"Why ever would she do that?"

"I think she knows much more about it than she's letting on. Perhaps she hoped I'd come to some harm."

"What happened?"

"I went poking about in the cloakroom. Did you know there's another cupboard off it?"

"I heard you tell the doctor. But I hadn't looked that far yet."

"Well, I opened the door into it. My torch didn't penetrate the darkness – then I got seized by the wrist and pulled forward into the dark –"

There was a sharp knock on the door and then it opened abruptly. Stephanie came in.

"Oh, *you're* here."

Sue stared at her. "What of it?"

"I think you'd better leave. Alistair and I have things to discuss."

Sue looked at Alistair. He was on the point of shrugging when he came to a decision. Why should this woman think she could rule his life?

"I don't see why she can't stay."

Stephanie sighed. "Oh, very well."

Alistair looked at her. "So?"

"I think there's something wrong with time."

Chapter 19

Alistair felt something tighten in the pit of his stomach. "Time?"

Stephanie looked at him piercingly. "I don't know how far it extends or whether this village is just in a bubble or maybe only part of it."

Sue grabbed her mobile out of her bag. There was definitely something odd about it.

Stephanie looked towards it. "You won't get a signal on that thing."

"Why not?"

"There's no coverage here for years yet."

"What?"

"What happened to you when you went into Alistair's house?"

"How do you know about that?" Sue asked, completely taken unawares.

"Just tell me."

"I heard a voice coming from downstairs. I came down and it seemed – it seemed to be coming from underneath the stairs."

Stephanie sat down on the only chair and bent forward, steepling her fingers under her nose. "Go on."

"I went into what I thought was a cupboard. I took a torch, but the beam didn't go anywhere. I expected to see a wall, but instead it was just darkness. Then something gripped me by the wrist and pulled me forward. In the distance was a light on the floor and as I went forward I saw a half circle of dark figures gathered round it. Then a voice spoke to me ... It said ... It said ... 'Tell him to remember January 11'."

Both Alistair and Stephanie breathed in sharply.

"Why January 11?" asked Alistair

Stephanie breathed out lengthily. "The day of the explosion."

Alistair stared at her. "What explosion? Where? When?"

"I see it all now."

Sue was getting angry. "What do you see?"

"A fracture in time."

Alistair got up from the bed. "Oh, this is ridiculous!"

"Whether you believe it or not it's happening. Miss Masters, have you noticed anything strange happening?"

Sue thought back. She knew nothing about biological warfare, but there were those two incidents at the railway station. And then there was something odd about her phone. She was sure it had looked different in the hospital and even by the river.

"When I was at Aberystwyth railway station I thought ... I thought for a moment ... when I was in the booking hall, that it all looked different and the ticket clerk wanted to be paid in pre-decimal currency. And then when the train came in it – was pulled by a steam engine ..."

"It's worse than I thought. There's nothing for it. You will have to come and stay with me while I think of what to do."

Sue stared at her open mouthed.

"You don't have to come, but Alistair must." Stephanie said icily.

Alistair sat down on the bed and squeezed Sue's hand. "I'd like you to come. I don't want to think of you being alone with all these strange people about."

"Okay," she said squeezing his hand back.

"I think we better go now before anything else happens."

"I'll just throw my stuff in a bag," Sue said.

"That goes for me too," Alistair said.

Stephanie sighed. "Don't be long."

As soon as they were ready she slightly lifted the grubby net curtain at the window and looked out sideways. "I can't see anyone. We'd better go now."

As silently as possible Alistair followed her down the stairs with Sue bringing up the rear.

Down in the hall Stephanie opened the front door with Sue behind.

Just as she was stepping over the threshold Alistair heard rapid footsteps behind him and he felt a sharp pain in his neck. His vision went fuzzy and he blacked out.

Sue turned round to find a thin sallow man with hooded eyes holding up a syringe ready to plunge it into her. She screamed.

Stephanie turned and ran at him from a standing start, kneeing him in the groin as he tried to plunge the syringe into her. He collapsed with a cry of pain.

Sue felt arms round her upper body and she kicked out viciously. Whoever it was grunted in pain and the arms let go – but only momentarily. A pad was clamped over her mouth. The moment she breathed in she felt darkness close upon her.

*****

Alistair awoke in a darkened room.

By turning his head he could see light outlining a door, but otherwise the gloom was pressing down on him.

He was lying flat and unable to move otherwise. He had been tied down to something, probably a bed, as it creaked as he tried to move. Sticky tape was over his mouth, but he could just about breathe through his nose.

His head thumped and his mouth was dry. How long had he been here? What time was it?

He felt hungry. That might mean something.

The last thing he remembered as he blacked out was Sue screaming.

What had happened to her? He was sure Stephanie could take care of herself.

He heard footsteps outside. They echoed – somewhere large and high and uncarpeted?

The door opened and someone in black robes with a deep hood shadowing his face stood regarding him. He or she came in, followed by two others. The door closed and a very low wattage bulb was switched on. He could still only see the mouths and chins of the people standing around him, one either side and one at the end of the bed. This last made a sign in the air which could be an upside down cross. Then it produced a bottle from a pouch at its waist, unscrewed the top, turned it upside down and waved it towards him. He felt a small amount of water splash on his face. The bottle was returned to the pouch

Slowly the three figures began to chant something in a low voice in an unknown language. Gradually their voices quickened and became louder until they ended up in a shout when all three hit their chests with a clenched fist.

Then one of them tore the tape off his mouth and thrust the open end of a small flask into his mouth. It tasted bitter. He began to feel woozy.

"Speak, Lamplighter."

"What are you talking about?" he muttered.

The man holding the flask turned to the speaker. "It has not yet begun to work."

"What have you given me?"

"Simply something to make you speak truly."

Alistair felt sick, but nothing came up.

"Speak, Lamplighter."

Their shapes began to waver and the voice seemed to come from a great distance, as if reverberating in a well.

"What about?"

"You can lead the trapped souls out. You have spoken to them, have you not?"

"No."

"Liar! "The man slapped him hard across the face. "What have they told you?"

"That they are cold, that's all."

"They know the future."

Alistair coughed. "Bully for them!" he said, miserably.

Dimly he saw one cowled figure turn to another. "He knows nothing. Give him to Barfog."

"He may yet remember."

"I say let the King of The Sea Trees make the decision."

There was a murmur of assent.

"Very well."

The tape was stuck back over his mouth and he fell into darkness.

*****

When he came round he could move, although stiffly. The room was dimly lit. The wooziness had left him but he was very tired and his limbs were leaden.

Who or what was 'Barfog' and who on earth was 'The King of The Sea Trees'?

With a huge effort he moved his legs and felt air move between them. He put his hand to his groin and found he was wearing a robe of some rough cloth but nothing else.

A sliding noise came from the door and a hole opened in it. Something covered it. Maybe they were spying on him.

"Let me out!" His voice sounded shrill and feeble.

The spy hole slid shut.

There was nothing for it but to lie there and see what would happen. He shivered in the damp cold seeping under the door.

What time was it? By holding the watch face up to the line of light seeping round the door he could just see that it was 9:30 at night.

He heard footsteps approaching.

A panel slid back at the bottom of the door, admitting enough light to show a metal plate with food on it being shoved through. The panel slid shut again.

'Feeding time at the zoo,' he thought grimly. The light level went up just enough to see it, but try as he might he couldn't get up and get it.

Again there were footsteps outside. A bolt was withdrawn and the door swung open, nudging the tray aside.

A man in a monk's habit came in, his hood low.

He looked round, picked up the tray and put it on Alistair's chest.

"Eat."

"Whatever it was you gave me I can hardly move."

The man grunted. "So, I ask you again, Lamplighter, what did they say?"

"Nothing. Just frightened me."

"But you will take us to them."

"I don't know how to."

"Very well. This Sue you have feelings for can tell us. You – you are disposable. A present for Barfog. At least I can give you a drink before you go."

Alistair felt his mouth expertly prised open and a glass of liquid poured in. He was forced to swallow.

*****

He woke up swaying from side to side. All about him were torches. He was strapped to some kind of wooden pallet – and seemed to be passing down an avenue of trees.

No – the trees were moving. They were branches of fir being carried upright by cloaked and cowled figures marching alongside.

He looked up. Stars glittered coldly overhead – only to be suddenly covered with wracks of cloud.

Ahead he could hear the sound of waves crashing on the shore. He was tilted downwards as the company slithered down a slope of slithering stones. Then the bier straightened up and what sounded like the soles of sandals slapped on wet sand.

The sound of the sea came nearer until those carrying him stopped abruptly.

Someone came towards him. Someone with the skeletal head of a deer with a huge rack of antlers. Now it all made sense. He remembered the skull on the wall at Digwell's house.

He was in the hands of the Greys. Digwell must be their leader.

The skull man raised both arms and, as the sleeves dropped down his arms, Alistair could see the half-moon tattoo on his upper arms.

The torches crackled and spat as the light flickered on the bony white skull and red eyes bored into him:

Drwy leithoedd ac elfennau
Straeon yn cael eu gorffen.
Tyfu fel afalle nau
Yn ei ddwylo; yr perllan

The voice of Archie Digwell, deeper than usual, fell on the salt laden air as it was repeated by the torchbearers in a deep mouthing:

> "The King Of The Sea Trees,
> Once a Keeper here before the
> Forest was submerged
> Doth in the time of harvest
> When tides are low,
> Walk round about the ruined oak
> With great ragged horns."

Two figures walked forward and handed him two daggers that glinted in the torchlight.

Turning slowly towards the waves Archie held them aloft against the sky.

As if on cue the clouds parted and a cold full moon stared down upon him, appearing under the arch of the two blades.

The skull shouted something unintelligible which was taken up by the assembled company who then walked forward carrying him – Archie leading them into the sea until they were up to their chests in the water.

Then they let go of the pallet and it floated free. They all turned with military precision and left him floating.

He was surprised that he did not sink. Then he began to move forward. The tide must be going out.

There was a great shout behind him and he looked down to see something silvery white rising towards him from the depths.

Chapter 20

All was silence after they'd gone.

Stephanie helped Sue up off the floor.

"Are you all right?" she asked

Sue dragged a hand over her face. "Feel a bit sick. Who were those people?"

"I was expecting this."

"Why?"

"There was nothing I could do except get you both to a place of safety."

Sue looked at her angrily. "Why?"

"It's October 31."

"So?"

"All Souls' Eve."

Sue was getting exasperated. "So?"

"The time of sacrifice."

"What?"

"To the water monster. Barfog."

Sue felt like grabbing this woman and giving her a good shake for being so obtuse. "WHAT?"

Stephanie just stood there, rocking slightly.

"So what do we do now?"

Stephanie gave her a thin smile.

"Does this thing exist?" Sue asked, exasperated.
"They think it does. That's enough for them."
"But does it?"
"Who can say?"
"Now look here …" Sue raised her hands.
"Don't get clever with me, young lady."
"Alistair told me about you – but being enigmatic doesn't cut any ice with me."
"What you've got to understand is that most of the villages are in on it. It has tendrils everywhere."
"So why didn't you keep him with you?"
Then the truth hit her.
"You used him as bait, didn't you?"
"They had to reveal themselves sooner or later."
"But what do we DO?"
Stephanie held her hand out. "Come with me."
"Where?"
"Somewhere they won't think of looking." Stephanie said.
"But where?"
"Young lady – you're in this, whether you like it or not. Just stop asking questions."
Sue crossed her arms over her chest. "If I'm going to come with you I need to know where."
"Somewhere safe, that's all I'm saying."
Sue realised she was getting nowhere with this woman. "All right – for the moment – all right."
Stephanie turned and went down the corridor and out of the back door. In the garden she strode over the grass towards a tall hedge at the bottom. Behind it was her old car. She inserted a key in the rusting lock and heaved the protesting driver's door open.
"Hop in. Right. Seatbelt on? Good. Hang on then."
The car crept out from behind the hedge into the lane and up to its junction with the High Street. Stephanie looked left and

right and then put her foot down. Sue felt herself jerked back in her seat. Where on earth was this mad old hag taking her?

The car shot up the road and, belying its age, took the bend where the road turned to the right almost on two wheels.

Soon they were travelling along a tunnel of trees when, with a deft pull down on the right hand of the steering wheel the car shot through an opening in the trees, over something that echoed metallically over a ditch, through an opening in a hedge and down a tiny track bounded by more high hedges. You could easily miss it if you didn't know it was there.

The hedge on the right stopped and Sue could he see a huge array of solar panels in serried ranks marching alongside the track.

With a lurch the car came to a halt behind a decrepit caravan shaded by a tree.

"Out." commanded Stephanie.

Sue unbuckled and heaved herself out of the depressed seat and onto the grass.

All was quiet except for the soughing of the wind in the trees and the occasional bleat of a sheep.

"Come on." Stephanie set off at a sharp pace towards another tree standing alone by a hedge. Alongside the hedge was a branch on the right held up by posts at the start of a path. Lashed to the end of the branch was an electric bell push.

"Best let him know we're coming."

"Who?"

"You'll see." She pressed the bell and started off down the steps. They led into a secluded dell. In it was a rather ramshackle bungalow with outbuildings and glasshouses beyond it. There were so many trees round it that it would be difficult to see from the air except in winter.

Stephanie went straight up to the door and thrust it open. "Hello? Anyone at home?"

Sue found herself in a sort of conservatory alongside the house. It was full of plants beginning to turn brown in the thin autumnal sunshine. The tomato plants looked crispy and yellowing.

There was a creaking sound coming up the corridor beyond an open door and a balding man in a wheelchair appeared. His concerned red and slightly veined face broke out into a huge smile.

"Stephanie! How lovely to see you! And who is this?"

"This is Sue. We've come to seek temporary sanctuary."

The man's face clouded again. "What sort of trouble you got yourself into this time, bach?"

"The Brotherhood."

"Oh, that's bad. That's very bad. Come away in anyway."

Sue followed them into a large kitchen diner with a window to the right. At the other end of the room were monitor screens on the wall covering all four compass points round the building and especially the entrance track. In front of them was a desk with electrical equipment strewn about.

"Cup of tea?" the man asked.

"Thanks, David. That would be lovely."

Stephanie settled herself down at the long scrubbed table as David busied himself with the kettle at the unit running the length of the room immediately to Sue's left.

She sat down on a thin cushion covering the seat of a grey wooden carved chair. "No sugar for me please."

"Right you are."

When the tea had been poured out into mugs David propelled himself on to the other side of the table next to Sue and peered at Stephanie.

"So, how can I help?"

Stephanie took a long gulp of tea. "They've kidnapped the Lamplighter."

"Oh, that's bad. That's very bad." David said, pursing his lips and sinking his chin onto his right hand.

"You want me to get some of the lads together?"

"No. Not yet. We need to know what's going on."

"Hmm." David looked round at the large clock on the wall. "Should be getting dark soon. You're thinking they're going to sacrifice him to Barfog, aren't you?"

"Seems likely."

The man tucked his bottom lip under his teeth and released them. "Need to know where they are, don't we? My guess is up at the dunes. It'll give them cover until they come out onto the beach by the estuary. Could put up a drone I suppose."

"How quiet is it?" asked Sue

"Oh, very." He smiled. "One of mine."

"I knew I'd come to the right place!" said Stephanie. "How soon can you get one up?"

"Oh, soon as you like!"

She didn't know why, but Sue thought she could trust this man. She also thought he would back her up if she had trouble with Stephanie.

"Do you know the neighbours in the semi next to Alistair?" said Sue.

"Angharad Rees, yes." The man said. "What about her?"

"I went round to see her – see if she knew where Alistair was. I came down from Birmingham. I felt he was in danger."

She saw Stephanie look round at her darkly. "How?"

Sue ignored her. "She didn't like me – wanted rid of me. Said I was an interloper. To go back to where I came from – so I left and went next door, up the steps at the back to see if I could see any sign of Alistair. While I was at the back door she came round into the yard and said I could wait in the house for him."

David and Stephanie exchanged glances. "Go on," he said.

"She let me in. I went upstairs and while I was there I heard a voice downstairs. I thought it was this Angharad so I came down. It seemed to be coming from underneath the stairs so I got a torch and went into the cloakroom. There was a door off the cloakroom and the voice was coming from there so I opened the door and –"

"Foolish child," Stephanie said angrily.

David looked angrily at her. "Let her speak."

"I went in. The torch beam just stopped in mid-air in the dark. There was no wall opposite, only blackness. Someone grabbed my wrist and pulled me in. I saw in the distance an oval of light. I walked forward and saw this circle surrounded by people in uniform and old-fashioned airmen's stuff – goggles and flying hats and ... and ... then this woman stepped into the light and said to tell him 'Beware the eleventh of January'. Then I woke up flat on my back in the cloakroom and I found this ... Angharad ... had locked me in the house."

The man looked across at Stephanie. "What do you make of that?"

Stephanie sucked her teeth. "I don't know. That date doesn't mean anything to me at the moment."

David put his mug down on the table. "I knew Angharad was mixed up in this somehow. Never trusted that woman." He looked out of the window. "It's getting dark, time to put Elsie up!"

"Elsie?" asked Sue.

"The drone."

They went outside into an outbuilding. David clicked on the light. The strip light banged several times and then clinked as a bluish green light flickered over the scene of Dexion metal shelving down the middle of the room and round the walls.

David wheeled himself over to a shelf and, heaving himself up, lifted off a propeller driven drone.

"Come here, my beauty."

He picked up a control pad with a built in screen, handed it to Sue and the drone to Stephanie. He settled himself back into the chair unsteadily.

"Hold that carefully Steph." he said, his voice echoing off the wall of the shed, "and bring her outside."

He got her to put it down on the cement yard.

"Right, Elsie my beauty. Let's see what you can do."

The drone lifted almost soundlessly into the air and sped off over the outbuildings becoming lost to view.

"Can you give me the controls Sue? Thanks. We're over the dunes now," said David looking at the screen, "I can see some lights. Looks like a gathering. Yup, that's them."

"The moon's coming out," said Stephanie.

Sue could see a full moon gradually coming up over the barn. She shivered.

"We'd better go," said Stephanie.

David waved them off. "Good luck! You're going to need it!"

Scouting round the outbuildings and glasshouses it wasn't far to the dunes. Within minutes they were crouching behind tufts of marram grass.

Stephanie whispered "See – there they are – grouped in a column two abreast within the confines of those two wooden lines of drowned forest – the moon is glistening off the wet sand showing up the black wood."

"Something's happening," whispered back Sue. "Someone's being brought forward on a sort of bier and there's a man with antlers on his head catching the moonlight – he's raising two daggers in a point above his head. We must do something!"

"I'm going in!" said Stephanie getting up into a crouch.

"But –"

Stephanie pulled the hood of her black robe she had borrowed from David over her head and stooping low, then lower, she seemed to flow shadowlike across the sand to the right of the column. Just before she reached the sea she cast off her robe and entered the waves.

Sue pulled her coat tightly round her and hunkered down, fearful of what would happen next.

*****

Alistair shivered uncontrollably as the bier floated on further out to sea, away from the chanting on the beach. What could he do, bound to the rough wood which was gradually sinking? He would have screamed, but for the gag in his mouth. What was it that Archie had said – a sacrifice to the water monster Barfog. Were they out of their minds?

He looked down into the depths of the water. There was something billowing white coming up to meet him – oh, God! Suppose they weren't mad and there really was …

With a gasp of breath whatever it was breached the surface and tossed its head. Spray slapped across his face and a voice said, "Can you move at all?"

Stephanie's voice!

All he could do was grunt.

"Right. Soon have you out of there."

Something flashed in the moonlight and he felt his bonds loosen. Now his gag was gone too.

"Just fall sideways off the wood and I'll catch you. Take a deep breath, we're going to dive!"

Strong hands pulled him down below the surface and he felt himself towed along. He couldn't keep this up – his body was frozen and he couldn't feel his hands and feet, but still the remorseless tugging pulled him downwards and along.

Just as he thought his chest would burst and he would have to take a breath to drown as salty liquid poured into him, he broke the surface.

Some distance away he heard shouts and then screams.

Deafening explosions rent the air. Bright flashes of light. He looked towards the beach. The column of men was scattering, dark forms fleeing in all directions as serpent tails of fire wove from above, landing on the beach where they didn't go out but burned brightly on the sand. One thought forced its way into his bludgeoned brain – Greek fire!

He was pulled to his feet and suddenly there was another person there. In the flashes of light he caught sight of Sue who dragged one of his arms around her shoulders while the other was looped over Stephanie's. Together they half ran, half dragged him across the sands and into the safety of the dunes.

Marram grass scratched his legs as he was lowered behind a dune. All three of them were out of breath.

Eventually, when Stephanie had regained the power of speech, she said "Brilliant wasn't it? David certainly knows how to lay on a show!"

Alistair coughed, spewing up seawater. "David, who's David?" His mouth was raw and the places where he had been tied, burned.

"We'll take you to him in a bit," Sue said looking out onto the beach where little fires burned fitfully. There was not a soul to be seen. The moonlight shivered on a deserted beach. All that could be heard was the gentle crash of the waves of the outgoing tide.

Alistair coughed again. "They were going to murder me! Sacrifice me to some water monster!" He turned to Stephanie. "Does it really exist?"

"Oh, it exists all right." She smiled wryly. "Just didn't get you today."

Alistair shivered.

"Come on," said Sue, "put this round you, it's not far to go."

A rough, smelly dark blanket was wrapped round him and together the three of them made slow progress out of the dunes across the road and into the fields beyond.

Later, sitting with a mug of hot tea with lots of sugar in it by a roaring Aga in David's kitchen, Alistair still couldn't believe it had all happened. David and Sue had attended to the cuts on his feet. David had lent him a spare watch as he was lost without one.

Sue looked at Stephanie incredulous, "So this archaeologist – this Archie – is the head of the Greys?"

"Along with a large part of the village, yes." said Stephanie, stretching out her long legs towards the heat.

Sue bent forward. "So what happens now?"

Stephanie clenched her bottom lip in her teeth and then relaxed momentarily. "Who knows? Having failed to make their sacrifice –and some may think that the fire was called down from heaven – they are scattered for the moment. But they'll regroup soon enough. And try again."

Alistair shivered despite the warmth. "But what do they want with me?"

Stephanie took a long pull at her mug of coffee. "They believe you're the gateway to another world. You're a Lamplighter, remember?"

"You mean there's more than one?" asked Sue

"There may be others in other parts of the world – but here there's only one at a time – so you're a valuable commodity."

"I don't like the sound of that!" Alistair said.

"Well, I'm afraid you'll just have to live with it."

Sue put down her mug on the table. "What sort of 'other world'?"

"The world of the dead. The Greys believe the dead can see into the future. If they can contact them who knows what would happen? They could shape things that are yet to happen."

"So what do we do?" asked Sue.

"It's against all I said but …" Stephanie sighed. "You've got to go back to the house and make contact with them somehow. Can you persuade the – the ghosts to move away? That corridor must be sealed up. I'm convinced something is happening to time."

"Sue can't go alone. I'm coming with you," Alistair said turning to Sue.

"You're hardly in a fit state …" Sue began.

David spoke for the first time. "If he wants to, he'd better go." They all turned towards him

"It's worse than I thought," he said, "Time is speeding up and it's going backwards."

Sue felt for her mobile phone. It was no longer there.

Chapter 21

"All this cloak and dagger stuff is getting on my nerves." Alistair said, as he crept along behind yet another hedge with Sue. His feet were wet. The bog was spongy underfoot, but it was the only place they were unlikely to be followed. There was no way you could get anything on it that wouldn't sink, except a noisy quad bike which would give away anyone following them.

After a night at David's and resting up most of today, they had left David and Stephanie planning their next move with strict instructions what to do when they got to Alistair's house.

It had been a long walk, or rather creep, across fields, eventually nipping across the railway line and into the more drained scrubland and then into the empty car park behind the hedge masking them from the road. Close by was the corner shop. All they had to do now was get across the road, over the short bridge fording the ditch, onto the caravan site and then onto the dog exercising field behind the row of houses that Alistair was in.

All the time it had been getting darker and now it was almost completely dark. The moon had gone down, hidden by cloud.

Sue peered out round the corner of the hedge and listened for traffic. All was quiet.

She looked back and waved Alistair forward. Together they ran at a crouch over the road and across the short, flat concrete bridge. Another sprint and they were in the dog walking field.

Keeping low they came to a halt behind a low blockwork concrete wall and looked out into the lane. An old-fashioned street lamp almost opposite the back of Alistair's house hardly illuminated the puddles in the lane.

None of the backs of the houses were lit.

Keeping low in the shadows behind the walls to the back yards they reached their goal and crept slowly into the yard, alert for any light suddenly coming on in any of the houses.

Sue produced a key to the back door and let them in.

The house smelt damp and musty.

There was just enough light from the street lamp to see across the kitchen to the doorway into the hall.

Once in the hall Sue found the torch on the hall table by feel and closed the door into the kitchen. She turned on the torch.

The brown paint and yellowing cream wallpaper hardly reflected any light.

Sue breathed in hard. "Ready?"

"As I'll ever be."

She opened the cloakroom door and they went in. It felt more claustrophobic than ever.

The door to the cupboard under the stairs stood open – and again the torch beam entered nothingness, disappearing into an inky void.

Far in the distance an ellipse of pale white light sprang up, hovering on what must be the floor. They made towards it.

Inside the circle of light they paused and listened. All around them was whispering – then slowly, hesitatingly, figures appeared out of the darkness – airmen wearing all manner of equipment from recognisably First World War to the strange and unfathomable. One looked modern in R.A.F. uniform.

"Who are you?" Sue dared to ask.

"Simon. Came down in 1989. Crash landed near here. Sorry."

"Why sorry?" asked Sue.

But the man didn't answer.

More servicemen arrived, some in army uniform stretching back and so far forward in time so as to be unrecognisable. They were all talking to each other and looking at Alistair. He shivered.

Then they fell silent.

A gap opened up in the ranks and someone came through. The tall woman with a gap toothed grin.

The woman in his dream.

Now he knew who she was.

Amelia Earhart.

"Hello, Alistair. We're sorry we gave you such a fright. We're not used to making contact with the living," she said in a soft mid-western accent. She turned to Sue, "Did you give him the message?"

"What message?" said Sue, faltering.

"Beware January 11."

"What do you mean, 'Beware January 11?'" Alistair said.

"That's all I can say. You can put right a great wrong."

"But …"

"Goodbye, Alistair."

Her voice echoed as the multitude faded into darkness.

He turned and his outstretched arm hit something hard. "Sue, put your torch on."

The light illuminated a wall in front of them and behind was the wooden wall of the inside of the cloakroom

Sue shivered. "It's so cold in here – let's get out."

Alistair shivered. "We never gave them our message."

"Too late now."

They came out into the hall.

It looked different.

There was no mirror on the wall or a table – only a high backed chair.

They went into the kitchen. In the dim light of day was a bread oven in the wall near the window – and next to it a fireplace. Next to that was an old-fashioned electric cooker with a rectangular solid hotplate at the back, a round one to the front.

A deep porcelain sink with cupboards underneath was on the opposite wall underneath a small window of opaque glass high up in the wall. Under the window looking out onto the yard was the same enamel topped table he'd bought with the house.

"I don't like this!" Sue said, her voice on the edge of a scream. "Say this isn't happening, Alistair!"

"I'm afraid it is. But when is this? It was night when we went in – now it's daylight."

There were a series of creaks from the hall as if someone was descending the stairs. The light went on in the hall and a man came in. He turned on the light.

He had several days' grey stubble and wore striped pyjamas with a grey woollen dressing gown over the top. It gaped open.

He walked straight past them, picked up a glass from the draining board and filled it from the tap. He drank it noisily, put it under the tap, rinsed it and put it back on the draining board. Then he turned abruptly towards the door, turned off the light and left. They heard him mounting the stairs and then all was silent.

Sue gasped. "Why didn't he see us?"

"Perhaps we're not here – yet."

"What do you mean?"

"Perhaps we're in transition from our time to another."

She reached out and took his hand. "I'm frightened."

"Me too. But we're here now – got to get on with it."

"What do you mean – from one time to another?"

"Well, look at this room. It's not our time – the layout's different, the cooker is different – that bread oven –"

"But it hasn't changed that much," she said

"Just shows how old the houses are. 1928 I think someone said. And look outside, beyond the yard – just grass and a hedge. No caravans. Sheep on the hill opposite. The door over there is half glazed – bottom half wood – top half little panes."

"I feel cold," she said. "Now I've got muscular pains – what's happening to us?" She buried her head in his shoulder. He clasped her tightly, stroking her hair.

As if someone had suddenly turned up the volume the silence gave way to birdsong. A car went past on the road at the front of the house. Weak sunshine came and went.

"I think we've arrived," he said.

Sue looked up at him. "We can't stay here!"

"No, you're right. But how are we going to get out? Your key won't fit that lock". He gestured to a large black mortise lock on the back door. "Let's go and have a look in the front room."

The furniture was the same, as were the sash windows in the bay, but the door into the front yard was half glazed in the same pattern as the back door. A large Welsh dresser was on the right-hand wall and a table was against the back wall. Ash and the remains of the ends of logs lay in the fire grate.

He went over to the windows in the bay and knelt on the window seat.

"Look – just a simple catch. You unscrew it then pull it like so and" – the top half of the window dropped down slightly – "all we have to do is slide up the bottom half and get out into the yard."

"I know. I did it to escape that awful woman. But suppose someone sees us getting out?" she said

"It's a chance we got to take. What other choice have we got?"

She nodded.

With several squeaks he hoisted the window up and got out, holding it up for Sue to get through. Then he gently let it down, gritting his teeth as it squeaked most of the way down.

"Come on," he said leading the way out of the gate way and across the road.

Sue paused. "Where's the wooden sea defence wall and the flower beds?"

In front of them was an undulating surface of flat and rough shaped stones which reached to a lip and then sloped steeply away to the beach and on the beach ...

Sue gripped his arm. "Look at all those sort of metal posts angled towards the sea – a whole forest of them!"

"They look like anti-tank defences. They must be expecting a seaborne invasion."

"You mean we're in some kind of war?" she said, that scream coming back into her voice.

"Looks like it, can't be the First – these houses wouldn't be here then."

The dawn was now far advanced. As Alistair turned he spotted someone coming towards them from his right – the direction of what could be a bus shelter or public conveniences.

He grabbed Sue and took her in a passionate embrace.

He heard the man go past.

Sue struggled free. "What was that all about?"

"Didn't you like it?"

She blushed to the roots of her hair. "Not out here!"

"I just had to hide us from the man going past. He looked sort of military."

"Oh," she said, crestfallen.

Alistair realised what she meant. He was never any good with women. "No, I didn't mean ... *'Now I've gone and made it worse!'* ... erm, we have to act like we belong here."

"That's going to be difficult. Girls didn't wear trousers in those days did they? And our materials look wrong for the time."

"I know. We'll just have to go to ground somewhere."

"But where?"

Alistair looked round him. "I dunno. Let's just keep walking."

The first thing he noticed was the absence of pavements. Sand was everywhere in small drifts across the road. Pebbles were up against the front walls of the houses. To his left the hangar-like holiday emporium had disappeared and in its place was a pink and cream building with wide semi-circular steps leading up to double entrance doors. Over the door was 'The Athlone Café' – doors firmly padlocked.

They went along a line of houses to their right which were all joined together, eventually coming to a bungalow at the end of the row. The house was end on to the road and the single window in it displayed packets and bottles of groceries. Over it was a sign 'The West End Stores'.

The door opened and a smartly dressed R.A.F. officer came out.

"Good morning," he said in clipped tones.

"Good morning," Alistair managed to stutter out.

The officer looked at him momentarily, a frown crossed his face and then he put his hand up to the brim of his hat in a sort of salute, gripped the edge and bowed slightly.

"Good morning, miss."

"Good morning, officer," said Sue, who had just time to collect herself.

The man turned and walked off. Then he stopped, turned and regarded them briefly and then started off again.

An awning over the front of the building sheltered a metal rack of newspapers attached to the white stucco wall by the door. It banged slightly against it in the breeze.

Alistair studied the masthead of one of them. The date was December 28th.

1944.

"We're in December 1944," he whispered to Sue without looking at her.

"No wonder I'm so cold – 1944! What are we going to do?"

"I don't know."

"We'll think of something!"

"Have you got any money?"

Sue unhitched her shoulder bag and had a look.

"About £20."

Alistair hit his forehead with his hand. "Stupid of me. It won't look like their money!"

Sue felt a scream bubbling up in her throat again.

Alistair frowned and looked round him quickly. "Come on, let's look down this lane, past the shop."

But there was nothing there but grass and hedges.

Alistair searched his memory. "There was a village hall up the village. It burned down in … but it'll be there now. And there's a Catholic church down by the railway …" He tailed off. "Get down!"

When she hesitated he pushed her down behind a hedge.

"Ow! That hurt! What's the matter?"

"M.Ps." he whispered.

"What?"

"Keep your voice down. Military police. Just saw them go past the end of the lane and in through the side door of the shop. That R.A.F. type must have tipped them off."

"What, already?"

"Look out! They're coming."

They heard the crunch of boots coming down the pebbled lane. Then they paused. Alistair looked between the foliage. They were sharing a cigarette and looking about them. They were talking, but too low for him to hear. Eventually they scrunched off up the lane, turn right up the village and disappeared.

Alistair realised he had been holding his breath all this time and his heart was banging painfully in his chest.

"Thank heavens that's over!" he said, feelingly. "We'll have to go through the fields round the back. Nearest place will be the Catholic church down by the railway."

Sue looked worried. "What if it's locked?"

"We'll cross that bridge when we come to it. Come on!"

Following much the same route they had the night before they came out on the other side of the track to the lane.

Alistair looked up and down it. "Can't risk going through that little gate next to the crossing gates. I bet the rusting spring holding it closed will make a heckuva noise if it's opened – might alert the crossing keeper in the house. Have to get under this two-strand wire fence and cross the track in the lea of this big hut, keep in its shadow and then run across the road to the church."

Sue nodded, unconvinced.

"You got a better plan?"

"No."

"Right, then."

High nettles and weeds shielded them from the keeper's house while Alistair held the bottom strand down with his foot and the top with his hand. Sue scrambled through. They made it over the track into the shadow of the black hut.

All was quiet. Looking up and down the lane they scuttled across the road to the door of the church.

It was open, but the sound of whistling came from inside.

Alistair heaved open one half of the outer doors and they found themselves in a small hall or porch with another set of double doors ahead. Opening one of them a crack he could see nothing but wooden chairs in rows and pallid walls. Then someone briefly crossed his line of sight. He closed the door again.

"It's a man. Might be a caretaker or something," he whispered

Sue grimaced. "What do we do?"

"Put on a bold front I s'pose." He opened the door and strode through hoping he looked like he was used to it.

The man looked up from his mop and bucket.

"Can I help you?"

Alistair thought fast. "Just looking for the vicar."

"Oh, you won't find him y'ere, not on a Thursday. He'll be preparin' the service fer tomorrow."

"Right. So where's the vicarage then?"

"You're not from roun' 'ere are you? And he's not the vicar. Didn't you see the sign outside? Catholic church this is. So where you from then?"

Caught off guard Alistair said, "Birmingham."

"Oh, a long way from home. How did you get your pass then?"

"Pass?"

"Travel pass. Take a lot of petrol to get down 'ere. You must be mighty important."

"Can't say," Sue suddenly spoke up. "War work." She patted the side of her nose with a finger.

"Ar. Well. That must account for your strange clobber, then."

"You could say," she said. "Well, we'll be going then."

"I could pass on a message if you give me a name," the man said.

"No, it's all right," said Alistair. He opened the door and Sue followed him out.

Sue grimaced when they were outside. "That went well."

Alistair clapped the side of his head, "Passes! Identity cards! If anyone asks for them we've had it!"

"Shit! We must stand out like a beacon."

"And we've just lit it. Look!" he said.

Military police, their white belts and straps across their chests shining in the sun, were coming down the road towards them.

Alistair knew it was no good running. One of them had already drawn his pistol. He waited patiently.

The taller one of the two immediately held out his hand. "Cards please."

"We haven't got them," said Sue

"You know it's an offence under regulations not to be carrying your cards at all times."

"We left them in the house by mistake."

"And what were you doing down by the railway line?" the shorter one asked.

"We just been in the church looking for Father –"

"Father who?" The taller one asked.

"The clergy house is that way," said the other one gesturing down the village. "I think you better come with us."

Alistair looked at him and shrugged.

They were marched up the lane around the corner to the left. Outside the dairy was a jeep and they were motioned into the back. One of the M.Ps. got in with them.

"Put these on please." He handed them two black blindfolds.

They put them on.

The jeep executed a quick three-point turn and soon the wind was whipping in their faces as the vehicle raced up the street heading north.

Alistair guessed it was about 10 minutes later that the road surface changed. The noise of smooth tarmac suddenly turned to a harsher note with the occasional jarring as if going over joints in the road and then over a corrugated surface. It reminded him of driving over concrete.

The jeep came to an abrupt halt with the engine idling. Voices of challenge and then repartee came and went and then there was a grating sound which he imagined could be a bar being raised or gate being opened.

The jeep started off again, still over the same corrugated surface, coming to a stop outside something from which sound was reflected.

The wind was strong here and carried a salt tang.

He heard the sound of the tailgate being dropped.

"This is where we get out, ladies and gentlemen."

Alistair got unsteadily to his feet and was helped down off the back. He heard Sue come off behind him.

"Forward six paces. Turn. Forward eight paces. Stop."

He heard the sound of a handle or knob being turned and entered an echoing room. His blindfold was removed and he found himself in a large bare room with two chairs on one side of a bare table and one chair on the other side.

"Sit."

They sat. The M.Ps. left the room.

"Where the hell is this place?" asked Sue.

"This must be the secret rocket testing range up at Ynyslas when it was operational."

"How do you know that?"

"I'm a journalist, remember?"

Sue suddenly put a finger up to her mouth indicating silence. "Suppose this place is bugged?" she whispered.

"Stupid me," he whispered back.

They sat still looking forward at the wooden wall in front of them. There was a door in the middle of it.

Alistair looked at his watch. 10:45. Their freedom hadn't lasted long.

He heard wind beat against the side of the hut and the walls creaked.

Gradually the fingers of his watch crawled round the dial to 12 o'clock. Alistair found he was getting cramp and the hard chair was making his bottom ache. He got up and walked round the room. The window had white strips stuck across all the panes in diagonal crosses, but showed nothing except grass, sky and hills in the distance.

Suddenly there was a deafening sound of a klaxon, and then another, followed by a thunderous *whoomp!* which made the whole room shake. There was a sound of running feet outside the hut – not just any running feet – but boots clumping along in unison.

Alistair was about to steal another look at his watch when there was a brief snatch of muffled conversation outside the door opposite and it opened. A familiar figure walked in.

Alistair gasped. Younger, maybe taller, with her short blond hair in a bob underneath her officer's hat, wearing a blue uniform with its hemline below the knee –

Stephanie Chambers.

At least it looked a lot like her. She was carrying a clipboard and a pen. She walked towards them, pulled out the chair and sat down opposite, put her clipboard on the table but did nothing else. Just sat there looking at them. Then she took her hat off and laid it on the table.

Eventually Alistair could stand it no longer.

"It's us, Stephanie, Alistair and Sue!"

The woman frowned. "Is this some new kind of trick? Ingratiate yourself with the enemy?"

"But it's us!"

She looked at him tight lipped. "Never seen you before."

Chapter 22

Alistair breathed in heavily "Sorry. You look just like someone we know."

"I see," she said in clipped tones. "You were found in the lane leading down to the railway line, having come out of the Catholic church apparently looking for the vicar. Surely you know Catholics don't have vicars. You've been poorly trained, though your English is good. Lived in England before the war?"

"Of course! We've always lived here!" Sue said.

"Name?"

"What?"

The officer looked up briefly, pen poised. "Name?"

Alistair took the initiative. "Alistair Powell."

"Real name?"

"That is my real name."

"Address?"

"Glaswern, Aberceldy, Ceredigion SY24 5LJ." It came out automatically and then he realised what he'd said.

She frowned. "What is Ceredigion? And this SY24 5LJ – some kind of code?"

"Yes, of course. It's a postcode."

"A post ... code." She repeated to herself writing it down slowly. "And the purpose of this 'post ... code'?"

"Helps the post be delivered more accurately"

She wrote this down methodically, looked at it – then –

"And you?"

"Susan Masters. Same address."

The officer's mouth twitched.

"And what are you doing here?"

"We live here!"

Now Stephanie sucked her bottom lip under her top teeth. She pointed her pen at them.

"But you don't know the name of the Catholic priest? And you don't have any identity cards?"

"We left them –" said Sue, but she was waved to silence.

"When were you dropped?"

Alistair leant forward "Dropped?"

The officer sighed. "Parachuted in!"

"Never."

"Came from the sea then, did you?"

"How?"

The officer appeared to lose patience. "By submarine."

"You have a very fanciful imagination officer. I bought my house in October – you can go and check with the Land ... of course you can't ..."

She leaned forward "Now who has a fanciful imagination? Which year?"

"1993."

"Preposterous! This must be some kind of new ploy of your masters – confuse the enemy with stuff straight out of science fiction! You'll be telling me you came from the future next!" She chuckled – then her face snapped back into a frown.

"You, Masters – take off your jacket."

"But ..." she said, looking towards Alistair.

"Take it off or two soldiers will come and take it off for you!" There was an edge to her voice.

Sue took off her red fleece, leant forward and put it on the table. The woman picked it up and fingered the fabric. "Your masters must be getting very slapdash. What is this word 'Berghaus'? German if ever I saw one."

"It's just the make of the jacket. Skiers wear them a lot or people go out hiking in them. I believe it's made out of recycled milk bottles."

The officer dropped it distastefully. "Whatever will they come up with next?"

The door opened behind her and a soldier came in and saluted. "Take this to the boffins and tell them to run tests as to its composition. I want the results within the hour."

"Yes, ma'am." He saluted smartly, turned on his heel and left.

Stephanie (if it was her) pursed her lips. "That'll be all for now. Someone will come and escort you to the cells." She picked up her clipboard, put her hat on and left the room.

Sue stared at Alistair. "No wonder she didn't believe me – it sounds fantastic even to me and we know it's true. I wonder what they'll make of my jacket?"

"Search me! But they'll eventually find there was nothing like it in this period in history."

Sue grasped his arm. "Don't you think they'll be even more convinced that we're Nazi spies? They'll just think that they've been working on some special material deep in the heart of Germany. You know they were terrified here that the Germans would create a hydrogen bomb before the Americans got there – so why not other things? Already V2's are dropping on London."

Alistair breathed in deeply. "I know –"

The door opened and two soldiers came in. "If you'll come with us, miss, sir?"

"Very polite aren't you?" said Alistair with a smile, but they remained stony faced.

They were marched out of the door they had come in and onto the road. A squad of soldiers marched past, eyes unwaveringly to the front. Another klaxon went off followed by another *Whoomp!* as a rocket soared off into the blue trailing an impressive trail of smoke.

They continued down the road towards the sea and the distant hills and then were wheeled right down a path between serried ranks of huts. Their escort paused in front of one.

"Halt!"

One of the soldiers leaned forward and opened the door and they went up a couple of steps and in.

Inside was a corridor running the length of the building and off it were several doors set into the wooden wall in front of them.

One of the soldiers marched left to the end door and unlocked it with a key from a bunch on a long chain. "You, miss, in here." She went in and he re-locked the door. "You, sir, in here."

He unlocked the door and thrust Alistair inside. He heard the door locked from the outside.

Alistair looked about him. There was a bunk bed to his left, a chair and a table under the window. A chamber pot was under the table, but no sign of any lavatory paper. Charming.

He lay down on the bed and knocked on the partition wooden wall.

"Can you hear me?" he said loudly.

Sue's voice came through rather muffled. "Can you see any microphones?"

Alistair glanced round the room. "No, nothing. But for all the noise we are making they could probably hear us outside!"

"I'll have a better look in a bit. Perhaps they're not set up for this sort of thing. They're not exactly escape proof," she said.

"No," he agreed, "Probably just for squaddies on a report or drunk."

"What are they doing here, Alistair?"

"Working on proximity bombs. The idea was to send up rockets in front of German bombers which would explode and hopefully set the targets on fire."

"Did they succeed?"

"Don't know. My research didn't stretch that far. It was all very secret – doubt if they let it go public even now."

"What's the time? My watch has stopped." Fear was creeping into her voice.

"3:30." he said.

"Wonder how long they'll keep us here?"

"No idea."

"I'm frozen. Wish I had my jacket," she said, a tremor in her voice.

"I'm sorry. I wish I could help. Doesn't seem to be any heating in this place. I should get into bed and pull the blanket up."

"I'm already there."

"Oh. Right. But that jacket, though. If they were to try and reproduce the technology it could change history."

"I thought about that. It's terrifying," she said, her teeth obviously chattering. There was a pause and then she said, "Have you noticed there are no light switches?"

"No. I hadn't. That's worrying – they could keep the lights on all night if they wanted. Standard procedure. Ever seen *The Ipcress File*?"

"No. And I don't want you telling me about it."

It gradually got dark until it was impossible to see anything outside – but the lights stayed resolutely on.

Chapter 23

It was very dark all around.

He was standing in a pool of light – and into that pool of light walked a tall thin woman with freckles on her nose. A short, boyish haircut curled over her forehead. Her mouth was tight-lipped. He knew she didn't like to smile because it showed the gap in her front top teeth. The newspaper article had said so.

"Hello Alistair." She said, in a soft Midwestern accent.

"Hello, Miss Earhart."

"You can call me Millie." The grey eyes regarded him somehow with amusement.

"Thank you, Millie."

"You know they used to call me 'Butters'- short for 'butterball' because I was so thin – like short people are called 'Lofty'?"

He didn't know what to say.

The grey eyes hardened. Dark smudges of tiredness showed under them.

"Do you know it got about that I was flying as a spy for the government and I was in the Pacific looking out for the Japs?"

"No, I didn't."

"It isn't true. I just wanted to be the first to fly round the world. You have to tell them that. I'm not a spy!" she said vehemently.

"Tell who?"

"My government – anybody. I don't want to be remembered as a spy!"

"What happened?"

"One of the fuel tanks wasn't completely filled. We just ran out of juice. We attempted two dead stick forced landings on the water. The waves were up to six feet high and it was difficult to judge our height above the sea. I hit my head on the radio. The metal box had sharp corners – and I must have knocked myself out. The plane must have hit the water and we drowned. Even if I had stalled at the correct height the plane would still have landed nose down tail up because of the weight of the engines. It would have been impossible to reach the emergency equipment in the tail. I don't want to be remembered as a spy. Put it right for me."

"Up!"

He was instantly awake, the light blinding him, causing dizziness.

"I said get up!" An arm pulled him out of bed.

"All right! All right! Keep your hair on."

A soldier was bending over him. "Officer wants to see you!"

He was marched out of the hut and down dark paths with white paint on either side which glowed in the moonlight.

They arrived at a large building he assumed he and Sue had entered in the morning and he was pushed into the interrogation room. The door slammed shut behind him.

There was nobody there.

There was just one chair now on his side of the table – but two on the other side. Who would be the other person?

He sat there for maybe half an hour constantly checking his watch to try and stay awake. Three in the morning.

The graveyard shift.

At 3.45 the door in front of him squeaked open and two officers came in – one who looked like a younger version of Stephanie and an American air force type by the look of him.

"This is Colonel Hayes," explained the Stephanie officer as they took their seats.

The Colonel laid his briefcase and hat on the table.

"So you're the Limey, huh? "

"Yes."

Hayes reached into the top pocket of his uniform jacket, pulled out a packet of Lucky Strike and shook it so that two filter tips extended. He held it out to Alistair.

"Smoke?"

"No, thanks."

"So," said Hayes, leaning back in his chair while lighting a cigarette and blowing smoke towards the ceiling, "You're from the future?"

"To you, yes. To me, no."

The Colonel leaned forward and blew smoke in Alistair's face. "You nuts or something? The future? This some Heinie trick or what?"

"I don't know what you mean?"

"I don't know what you mean," Hayes repeated in a passable English posh accident. He leaned forward further and slammed a meaty fist down on the table. "Okay, Buster, just you tell me one important thing that happens in the future."

"I can't tell you that. It could change history."

"Oh, right ... very convenient. So why should we believe you?"

"You had a look at Sue's jacket. What do you think?"

"He has a point, Colonel," Not Stephanie said.

The Colonel stubbed out his cigarette on the table, much to Stephanie's obvious annoyance. His mouth twitched. "Go on. Give us one date. One lousy date."

Alistair looked at them. The date that was really close now. One he had been warned of, but about which he knew nothing.

"How about January 11?"

Both officers looked at each other in horror.

Alistair smiled in spite of himself. "I see I've touched a nerve."

They got up as one and went out through the door in front of them.

Well, thought Alistair, whatever happens then must be mighty important.

*****

Sue woke up suddenly. What was that?

There was a tap on the window, then another. She got up and squinted through the two panes of glass that had not been covered by a board.

A torch shone in her face.

A male voice said, "Stand back, I'm going to break the glass."

"What?"

"Ready?"

Sue stood back. There was a tinkle as the shards hit the floor and a screwdriver was handed through.

"Unscrew the boards over the window and then release the catch. Get up onto the sill and drop down. I won't let you fall. Here's the torch."

"Who are you?"

"Tell you when we've got away."

Working feverishly, torch in hand, she unscrewed the board and carefully lifted it down, leaning it against the wall.

She tucked the torch into the waistband of her trousers, released the window catch and heaved herself up onto the sill.

"Where are you?" she whispered.

"Just below you."

"Okay. I'm coming."

She dropped seemingly a long way in the dark, but strong arms grabbed her underneath her arms and steadied her upright.

"Follow me."

Whoever it was started running at a crouch along the line of the huts outlined in the moonlight.

Twisting and turning among ranks of huts, keeping low under curtained windows, Sue found herself outside a hut where her rescuer unlocked the door and went in. She closed the door behind her.

The light came on in a sparsely furnished sitting room with threadbare armchairs and a standard lamp. Something that she recognised as a brown Bakelite valve radio was on a shelf.

She turned to see her rescuer –

The doctor! It must be him. A younger version – yes, but it must be the Borth GP, the same eyes, same studied expression – his hair mid brown instead of grey – but the same man who would examine her in the surgery when they were hiding from the man in the bus.

"I know you!" she said without thinking.

The man's forehead creased. "How so?"

"You're a doctor, aren't you?"

"Yes – but how did you know?"

Sue breathed out. "It's complicated."

"Would you like some tea and tell me about it?"

"Please."

"Rightho then. Sugar?"

"No, thanks."

The doctor went into the kitchen and Sue sat down, the muscles in her legs still jittering after all that frightening exercise. The chair's springs were on the way out and the arms were worn.

The man came back in and put down a tray containing the tea things on a low table.

"So why did you rescue me?"

"Bad things are afoot. I thought you might know something."

"You think I'm a spy?"

He sat down opposite with a cup of tea and regarded her, frowning.

"And aren't you?"

"'Course I'm bloody not!"

"So why are you here?"

"Got arrested." She sipped her tea.

"Who by?"

"Military police." Somehow she knew she could trust him. "We were looking for somewhere to hide."

"What from?"

"You're not going to believe this."

"Try me," he said leaning back in his chair and taking a sip of tea.

"We got back to this house on the sea front owned by my friend, went into this room under the stairs and when we came out … We had gone back in time." She saw him frowning again. "See – I told you wouldn't believe me."

"Oh, I believe you all right."

She sat bolt upright. "Why?"

"I was visiting a patient in the house next door – the other half of your friend's semi. I came out just as you and a man were clambering out of the sitting room window. You both looked worried and lost. Then you went across the road and saw the sea defences on the beach. Spies would have known about them. Your reactions were all wrong. So what are you?"

"Accidental travellers from the future."

"As I thought. There's always been something odd about that house. The way it was designed. Jones was a bit weird. Had to treat him several times. I told Captain Chambers you weren't spies –"

"So it is Stephanie!"

"What do you mean?"

"She interviewed us, but pretended not to know us."

"Maybe because she hasn't met you yet?"

"You seem to be very well-adjusted to all this, doctor …"
"Cynwy Davies."
It is him, thought Sue.
Davies just smiled.
'*There's more to him than meets the eye,*' she thought.
"Strange things have been happening round here. You're not here for a particular date are you?"
"Yes. January 11. How did you know?"
"I didn't know. But now it's too clear. There have been whispers that the day after tomorrow they are going to test the rocket that will deliver the bomb."

Chapter 24

Alistair stared at the ceiling, bored out of his mind. How long had he been here? At one time he'd woken up to find himself on the floor with no idea how he'd got there. Must've fallen asleep on the hard chair and toppled off. It was cold on the floor and draughty. He got back on the chair again. He looked at his watch. It had stopped.

Must be quite late or quite early depending on which way you looked at it. The dark outside the window was gradually turning grey and the overhead light bulb seemed dimmer.

A bloke could go mad sitting here.

The door opposite opened abruptly and Not Stephanie strode in. In one hand was the ubiquitous clipboard – in the other was a paper carrier bag.

She put down the bag and the clipboard on the table, pulled out a chair, sat down and looked at him for a long moment. Her mouth twitched. She grasped the bag and took out something. Sue's jacket.

"What can you tell me about this?"

"It's Sue's jacket. You saw her take it off."

Not Stephanie's mouth twitched again and she leaned back, looked at the ceiling and exhaled slowly. Then she snapped back and looked at him full in the face.

"No more games."

"What games?" he asked.

"We've just run a series of tests on this. The boffins tell me it's made of a combination of materials, some of which is glass. How did she come by it?"

"You better ask her. I expect she bought it from a shop."

"Bought it from a shop? When?"

"I dunno. In the 1990s I suppose."

"You do know what year this is?"

"'Course I do."

"So?"

"1944."

"Yet you persist in this fiction that you're from the future? So tell me something that happens in the future?"

"I've already done that. And yet you still don't believe me. If I tell you something significant it could change history."

"Okay. Something that wouldn't change it."

Alistair thought carefully. Whatever could it be? Anything could start it off. I know … "The war in Europe ends in 1945."

"And?"

"Hitler dies."

"How?"

"Can't tell you that."

Again the grimace.

"You're too dangerous to keep here. With what you know. The Americans want to be far less gentle – in fact not gentle at all. Sodium Pentathol – that sort of thing."

"You mean you believe me?"

"This jacket is all the proof I need. Colonel Hayes thinks it's Nazi research, but he can't make his mind up whether you are a total idiot or a spy or somehow both. However, our intelligence doesn't bear out that it's Nazi research. We're having to think the unthinkable. This is difficult."

"So you'll let me go?"

"Of course not. You're going to escape."

"How?"

"We use DUKWs to recover spent rocket parts from the estuary, or balloons or parachutes – the locals are always trying to nick them for silk underwear and the like. I can arrange for one of them to be fuelled up and the ignition key left somewhere you could find it."

"What are DUKWs?"

"Ah, I see you don't know everything," Not Stephanie said with quiet satisfaction. "'Ducks'. Converted six-wheel American army trucks that can operate on land or on the water by switching the transmission to a propeller. A lot of them are parked on the perimeter of the camp by the forward observation post."

"What about Sue? I'm not going without her."

"Oh, yes, Sue. Too clever for her own good. Sentry found her room unoccupied. I'm the only one that knows that. For the moment."

"So you want rid of us?"

"Yes. That's what I'm saying. We can't have you locked up indefinitely – or kill you – something's bound to leak out. And I'm averse to letting the Americans experiment on you. "

"That's very comforting."

"Listen, Mr Powell, you just don't get it do you?" Not Stephanie leaned forward and said acidly, "This is total war. The Nazis don't care what they do and we shouldn't either. Here, sign this" – she shoved the clipboard towards him. "Official Secrets Act. If anything – anything at all – leaks out you will be hunted down, tried and executed as enemies of the king. Have you got that?"

"I've got it."

Alistair signed. He was sure she meant every word. He slid the clipboard back across to her.

"Right. Go and find Miss Masters and get the hell off this base. This is the number of the duck. Be there at 0600. I will create a diversion to cover the noise of your departure. Those beasts are bloody noisy. Dismissed."

"Yes, sir, madam."

Not Stephanie's mouth twitched. She got up turned smartly and left, leaving him with the bag.

0600. What was the time now? I haven't got a clue.

*****

Sue gripped the arm of her chair. "The bomb?"

"Anthrax." Dr Davies replied.

"But that's against the Geneva Convention and stuff isn't it?"

"This is total war, young lady. It's the Geneva Protocol anyway – a common mistake to make. The Japs are hard at it and we are as well at Porton Down. And you and I are going to stop it."

Sue nearly barked with laughter. "The two of us? How?"

"The war will be over one day. Do you want this on our conscience? All we have to do now is slow it down a bit. Sabotage the delivery system."

There was a tap on the window and both of them jumped, jerking towards the curtains. Sue was up before she could think and twitched a corner of the curtain aside. She could just make out Alistair standing below with a stick. He gestured he wanted to come in.

"Who is it?"

"Friend of mine. Don't know how he got out – but we must let him in at once."

"Impossible."

"Well, I'm going to do it."

The Doctor launched himself towards her, but she was too quick for him, leaving him lying on the carpet. She ran to the door and wrenched it open. Alistair practically fell in.

"What's the time?"
Sue was taken aback "What? I don't know."
The doctor was already in the hall.
"What's the time?" they said together.
"What?" He looked at his watch. "20 to 6 – why?"
"Do you know where the ducks are?" asked Alistair breathlessly.
The doctor was going red in the face. "Stop this. I demand an explanation!"
Alistair looked at Sue. "We're being let escape – Not Stephanie is going to arrange a diversion – we're going to get away across the estuary."
The doctor grabbed Sue's hand. "Madness! The currents will kill you."
"You got a better idea?" Alistair said.
The doctor looked into Alistair's face. "What time have you got to be there?"
"0600 she said."
"So you're not going to help me then, young lady?"
"No not yet – we got to get out of this mess first."
The doctor sighed heavily. "Come on then."
A sea fret had swept in from the estuary making it difficult to see, but the doctor strode into it confidently. Alistair took hold of Sue's hand and pulled her after him.
It seemed to him that they had been walking for far longer than was necessary to reach the outskirts of the camp, but he couldn't tell in this fog.
Then tall fuzzy shadows loomed up. They must be more than 8 feet high Alistair thought. He got the piece of paper with the registration number on it out of his pocket, held it up close to his eyes and then hunted along the row of monsters. The ink on the paper was beginning to run in the water laden air. Soon it would be unreadable. Ah, there it was.

He turned to Sue, who was wiping her glasses to get rid of the mist. "We're here."

Sue looked up. "It looks awfully high."

"I'll give you a hand up if you like."

A look of steel came into her face. "I'll be all right, thank you," she said tightly.

Alistair looked round for the doctor but he had vanished into the murk.

"Looks like we're on our own," he said, looking at Sue. "You ever driven one of these things?"

"No, you?"

"Nope. I'll go up first. Hope the keys are easy to find."

He heaved himself up using several knobbly ledges built into the dark green metal. It was difficult pulling the door open towards him without falling backwards onto the ground, but he managed it.

Inside were a couple of basic metal seats with round holes punched in them. He moved across to the other door and thrust it open, looking down at Sue. "Go round the other side." She vanished, reappearing on the passenger side. "Need a hand up?"

"Okay. It's higher up than I thought."

He heaved her up into the cabin.

"Not exactly luxurious is it?" he said, when she was settled in her seat. "I found the key lodged under the seat."

He turned the key hoping it would fire first time. It didn't. The noise of the engine turning over was deafening. Surely someone would come running?

Just then there was a violent explosion and flares could be dimly seen. Soon dense black smoke began rolling towards them.

He turned the ignition again. This time it fired – but which way was the water? And what to do when they got there? He put the interior light on. Between the seats were separate controls for engaging the propeller and deflating and inflating the tyres.

"Right. Here goes nothing!" He gunned the engine and put the windscreen wipers on.

Ponderously the steel monster moved forward. It was making a tremendous din. Surely somebody would come? He imagined, even now, warning shots whining overhead.

But nothing happened.

They were suddenly encased in thick black smoke.

Ahead, in the broadening dawn he could just see the mist curling, hovering over the water underneath the black smoke. In a moment they were in and he turned on the propeller.

He turned to Sue. "All right?"

Sue nodded. Her face was grim, staring out in front of her. Any moment he expected the tug of the tide, but there was very little drift. Perhaps Not Stephanie had looked at the tide tables and judged when the flow down the river balanced the tide coming the other way.

From the sound of the engine they must be entering deep water. He increased the revs and the engine responded with a throaty roar. But were they headed in the right direction? He looked up above the windscreen.

There was a bulb in which hovered a compass. They were heading north east and the drift was increasing. They should, on his reckoning, be heading due north. Where were the rudder controls? Ah, there they were! Now they were heading north, but he could feel the machine drifting to his left.

How much further? If only he had a working watch! Got to keep going.

A rock wall loomed up to his left and the DUKW was swept against it, almost turning round as it got caught in the eddy caused by the water swirling past it. The collision was bone jarring. He squeezed the maximum out of the engine and with a roar the tyres gripped something.

He turned off the propeller and put the wheels into forward traction. They seem to be going up an underwater ramp.

And then, just out of the water, the engine failed. He pulled hard on the hand brake expecting the machine to start slithering backwards. There was an ominous creaking and jarring.

"We got to get out! She's not going to hold. Tide's going out!" he said breathlessly.

He opened the door and jumped down into the water. Staggering a bit he heard a splash as Sue landed on the other side.

He was waist deep in cold seawater, seaweed washing up and down around him. The sound of the waves echoed against what must be harbour walls.

He waded round to the other side to see Sue clinging to the bodywork, submerged up to her shoulders.

He hung onto the bumper with one hand and stretched out his left. She grabbed it and together they scrabbled round the front until they were in the lee of the dark wall, seaweed hanging from every crevice. A sharp tang of salt was in the air.

With a tearing screech the DUKW slid backwards and disappeared into the fog.

Too cold and exhausted for words he pulled Sue up the underwater ramp and together they inched up the wall, hand over hand, scraping them on the rough surface.

At the top they lay down on the cobbles, gasping for breath.

A breeze sprang up and gradually the fog dissipated, showing they were in a wide roadway leading down into the water. A long arm of the harbour wall was thrust out into the sea and it was against this that the DUKW had collided. If the wall had been any shorter they would surely have been carried out to sea and probably drowned in the vicious battleground where sea and river met.

There was nobody about. Windows were curtained and there was not a sign of a light anywhere.

Alistair's breath slowed and, as it did, the real world sounds began to intrude – and into that world came a strangled rumble, bounce and squeak as of some aged protesting machinery in need of oil.

Chapter 25

Alistair sat up as round the corner of a building came a thin gaunt man in black, riding out of the mist on a rusting sit-up-and-beg bicycle.

He saw Alistair at the same time as Alistair saw him. The man quickly dismounted, leaning his ancient machine against the wall and ran stiffly towards him. At this distance there was no mistaking the dog collar.

"Are you all right, sir? And the young lady?" asked the vicar.

Alistair raised himself up into a sitting position "We're all right – just out of breath."

"I think you'd better tell me all about it. The vicarage's just round the corner. My housekeeper will have a fire going in the kitchen. Come on!"

He went over to the wall and wheeled the protesting machine towards them. "Got this out of the woodshed – scarcity of petrol you know." He smiled and his face became even more skull-like, showing big teeth. "Just follow me!" He set off up a side street which sloped away from the harbour.

Alistair looked at Sue, who nodded.

Thankfully the house wasn't far away and as soon as they stepped through the front door foetid heat enveloped them. The priest led them through to the kitchen at the back where a fire blazed. A rotund woman was bending over a large blackened pot in which something bubbled on the Aga.

"What yow got there, vicar? More waifs and strays?" It was a strong Birmingham accent.

"Can you get them some blankets? It's cold and wet out there."

"And yow should be wearing your coat, Your Holiness – you'll catch your death!"

Alistair grinned inwardly. It was plain she was not from round here. That could be a bonus. The woman bustled out of the room.

They sat on wooden chairs round the fire, steaming laundry hanging from a rack overhead. The pale walls streamed with condensation.

"Nothing like it for warming the cockles," said the vicar, holding his hands out to the blaze. "I'm Michael, by the way – and you are?"

"David and Fliss," said Alistair quickly. He didn't want to give away too much at this stage.

"So what were you doing down by the harbour? You aren't spies are you?" Michael asked, half mockingly.

"Our boat sank."

"What on earth were you doing out in a boat in this fog? Don't you know that the estuary's lethal at the best of times?"

"Our yacht got loose from its moorings and drifted off. We thought we'd try and get it back – which was stupid, really."

"I'll say it was! Ah, thank you Mary!" He took two rough-looking grey blankets from the housekeeper, who went back to stirring the contents of the saucepan. "Put them on! Put them on! Now you look like you could do with something warm. How about a mug of tea and a bowl of porridge – keep out the cold!"

Mary served them bowls of steaming oats and thick mugs of tea. Having got round those Alistair began to feel a bit better. He couldn't remember when he'd last eaten. Sue was beginning to look a bit less pale.

The vicar looked round. The housekeeper had gone.

"Okay you two – what really happened?"

"What I said."

The vicar looked at him a long time and then shook his head. "Not sure I can be trusted, eh?"

Alistair looked at Sue. She nodded.

The vicar leaned back and steepled his fingers under his nose. He breathed out slowly.

"I'm not sure anyone can be trusted in this war," Alistair said, heavily.

The man's lips twitched. "Got to trust someone."

Sue suddenly leant forward and said quietly, "We've come from the base."

"Have you now? We saw strange lights from there before the fog really closed in. You weren't anything to do with those were you?"

"No," said Alistair, "We don't know what they were either."

"Hmm. So?"

"They arrested us in the village as spies and brought us to the camp."

"And you escaped?"

"Yes." Sue said softly.

"Won't they come looking for you as soon as the fog clears?"

"I don't think so," said Alistair. "Someone was glad to be rid of us."

"Well, you are an enigma and no mistake! And where do you plan to go now?"

"We don't know," said Alistair. "But we must get back to Aberceldy."

Michael leant forward. "It's a long way – back east along the river right up as far as Pontceldy where there is a bridge over the river and then back through and round until you hit the road across the marsh to the long road running along by the sea."

"How far?"

"About 30 miles."

Alistair looked at Sue. They were never going to make it on foot. Using public transport – if there was any – might arouse suspicion.

It was if the vicar could read their thoughts. "You'll have to change out of those clothes. They're a right giveaway."

Sue leaned forward. "In what way?"

"Come on, young lady! I've never seen a red jacket like that before! What is it?"

"It's a fleece."

"Doesn't look woolly to me. Look, I've got some fairly non-decrepit baggy clothes that would probably fit both of you. You could put them over the top. You game?"

Alistair looked at Sue and they both grinned at the vicar.

Later, wearing baggy flannels and shapeless sweaters with Sue's unruly hair rammed down with a tightfitting cap they were ready to leave – but where had the vicar gone?

The answer came from the sound of what could be a low power lawnmower. The vicar came into the hall from the street. Behind him was the all pervasive mist and something black.

"Come on then. No use hanging about!"

Surprised, Alistair said "You're taking us?"

"How else will you get there? It'll be a bit of a squeeze in the Austin but we'll manage."

He led the way out to what Alistair could see was an Austin Seven sitting alone by the roadside purring away like a sewing machine.

They squeezed in – Alistair in the front, Sue in the back on the cracked brown leather seats, much worn.

Borderlands

The slits in the headlights did not give out much light, but the vicar nosed out surely onto the open road.

Alistair peered through the windscreen. "You get fogs like this often?"

"Quite often – comes off the river – especially when the weather is calm and you get different temperatures between the sea and the river. I'm used to visiting parishioners in it. Takes longer, but we get there in the end."

The fog closed round them and they could be anywhere – in another world even.

They'd been going some time with the vicar turned on the radio and the car was flooded with dance music. "Usually have the radio on when I'm out. Helps the journey seem shorter."

The clock on the dashboard, which looked like an independent clockwork device, said 10.30.

At 10.35 the radio started behaving strangely fading in and out and buzzing with atmospherics.

"Gets like that some sometimes," said the vicar peering forward and using the windscreen wipers intermittently, "something to do with the hills."

Then, from overhead, came the droning sound of an engine. Whatever it was, it was perilously low.

Over the atmospherics Alistair heard a distorted female voice coming and going interspersed with noise. "SOS, SOS, SOS, KHAQQ, KHAQQ."

"Stop the car!" shouted Alistair, staring up through the windscreen, straining to see through the fog.

The droning overhead continued. Then, just for a few seconds, the fog parted and there was the grey outline of a plane. Alistair froze. Could it be? Could it be? It looked like it.

The picture in the newspaper.

A Lockheed Electra 10 – E.

The plane that disappeared over the Pacific. The plane with Amelia Earhart in it.

And her call sign.

He shivered.

Just before it disappeared he could see, or thought he could see, the underside of the wings and NR T6020 in huge black letters and numerals or was it MR I 6020?

He had no doubt about it. It was her plane.

A twin engined turboprop with engines either side of the cabin that was mounted higher than them.

A faint hiss and crackle of static and then quite clearly her voice "Alistair."

He wrenched open the door and staggered out into the fog, looking upward.

But it had gone.

The sound, the grey shadow, everything. He groped his way back to the car and closed the door. The vicar looked at him narrowly.

"What was all that about?"

Alistair continued to look up through the windscreen. "Do you believe in ghosts?"

"Oh, yes, been called to do one or two exorcisms."

"Really?" piped up Sue from the back seat.

"Yes, really," said the vicar, drily. "So what's all this about?"

"Just thought I saw something that's all."

The Vicar continued to look at him. "What sort of something?"

Alistair looked at the vicar." A plane out of history. Did you hear anything come over the radio like a call sign?"

"No, I didn't hear anything, just atmospherics. Are you feeling all right?"

"Not really."

"Well you have had a nasty escape." He let the car into gear and continued on down the road. "But I don't believe you are who you say you are. Why are you here?"

"We don't know," said Alistair.

"Have you heard these voices before?"

'*He thinks we're mad*,' thought Alistair. He decided to tell some of the truth. He is a vicar after all.

"Yes, I have."

"Where?"

"In the house I've just bought."

"And what did these voices say?"

Sue couldn't stop herself. "Beware January the 11th."

"But that's today!"

"We know," she said.

"And what do you expect to happen?"

"We don't know!" said Alistair.

The vicar grunted but said nothing. Then, "Ah, here's the turn off."

That seemed to put an end to the conversation.

Going along at a steady pace with someone who knew what they were doing, where to go and with nothing to look at but fog Alistair found himself rolled into a dream from where he passed into sleep.

"We're here," the vicar said.

"Wha?" said Alistair dragging himself awake. He looked round. Sue was fast asleep.

The passenger door was pulled open next to him. Strong hands reached in and grabbed him, dragging him out and propelling him a short distance through a door. He heard Sue scream as he was dragged through another door and dumped in a chair. Moments later Sue was deposited in a chair next to him.

Alistair looked about him. In the dimness of light coming through grimy windows he could see he was in a church. Up on the wall behind the altar was a cross.

It was upside down.

Chapter 26

Below the cross was an altar draped in black. A gold crescent moon with four stars within its horns shone dully on its front.

'The same tattoos as Sue or I have seen on the psychology student's arm and Ben the bus driver', Alistair thought.

Two cloaked and cowled figures sat either side of them, but faced forward saying nothing.

Alistair looked round at Sue. She was alabaster pale and tears were streaming down her face. He reached out and took hold of her nearest hand, squeezing it tightly.

"What ... What are they going to do to us?" she breathed in a terrified whisper.

"I don't know. Just don't let go of my hand, okay?"

She nodded and then went rigid. He could feel an electric charge surging through him from her hand.

"Something's coming. I can ... I can feel it."

"Well, well, well. Who have we here?"

Archie's voice came from behind. Alistair heard footsteps on the bare floor coming round them.

The archaeologist grinned at him from beneath his black hood. "Escaped from me once before, didn't you Mr. Powell? There'll be no drones or fancy fireworks to save you this time."

Alistair was stunned. "What? But that was … that was … that is … 50 years in the future!"

"Quite so, dear boy. Quite so." Archie stepped forward and slapped him hard across the face. "'Beware January 11' – and you said they hadn't told you anything. Well, this time you will tell us everything. Prepare her for the ceremony!"

The man on Sue's right took hold of her hand next to him and was about to pull her to her feet when a low growling came from overhead, getting louder and louder.

"It's here!" screamed Sue.

Alistair dragged her to her feet. "Run!"

A loud whistling shriek came from above as they threw themselves through the open door into the tiny hall. The air turned to dust and fire.

*****

Deafened, Alistair gradually returned to consciousness, coughing, covered in bits of plaster and dust. The ceiling of the small room had saved them, but it was bulging, broken laths hanging down. Ominous creaking was coming from above.

A heavy post was lying diagonally across the door into the hall, flames licking up it, blocking any view of the inside.

Tentatively, he turned over to find Sue under a pew against the wall to his right, blood trickling from her forehead, making a pathway down the plaster dust coating her face.

"Sue! Sue! Are you all right?"

She didn't move. He heaved himself to his feet, broken brick biting into his hands, and trod unsteadily over the heaps of plaster, and debris. Bending down pain shot up his back. He stroked her cheek and her eyelids flickered up, but she didn't say anything. Then, with a great effort, she whispered something. He knelt down despite the pain.

"What is it?"

"She ... she must have led them here," she said, her eyes closing again.

Alistair looked up. The roof above them was beginning to give way. How long before it fell in? Perhaps something had fallen from above on it. The heat was becoming more intense.

He scrabbled around to clear a path amongst the broken brick, his fingers bleeding. He would have to move her, no matter what. The whole building could be about to collapse.

He pulled her from beneath the pew as gently as possible and carried her out into the fresh air. She seemed as light as thistledown.

Laying her on the grass at the side of the parking space outside the church he collapsed beside her, coughing wildly.

The next thing he knew was someone shaking him. He looked up. Two soldiers in dark blue with red cross armbands round their upper arms looked down at him.

"Are you all right sir?"

"I don't know," he choked out. Tried to get up and sank back.

Next thing he was being lifted onto an evil smelling fabric structure. He dimly saw Sue go past, carried in one as well.

Then he was inside an ambulance. The door slammed shut and the vehicle was bouncing away along the road. It turned sharply.

'*We must be going back to the base ...*' he thought dimly. '*The place we've just escaped from.*'

The thought galvanised him into action. He rolled over and looked across to the other stretcher. Sue appeared to be asleep.

"Sue?" he whispered loudly, "Sue?"

Her eyelids slowly opened. "What's going on?" she coughed.

"The R.A.F's. caught up with us again – must be going back to the camp."

"Oh, God. What will they do to us this time?"

"I dread to think. Pretend to be more ill than you are – give us time to think."

The ambulance was slowing down now and came to a halt. He could hear shouts and the rusty creak of a barrier being raised. The vehicle lurched forward as the clutch was inexpertly used and the blowback of exhaust entered the inside making them both cough.

Not much further on it came to a halt and the doors were flung open. Alistair saw through half closed eyes a man in a white coat look in. He gestured to someone out of sight and two men in blue uniforms climbed in and heaved out the stretcher Alistair was on.

He was about to be carried away when they stopped, arrested by furious barking. He could see one of them look round and then the other. Sue was being unloaded and a dog handler was desperately hanging on to the lead of a ferocious-looking Alsatian.

Suddenly it lunged forward and bit Sue's arm that was hanging over the side of the stretcher.

"Spike! Spike! Calm down boy! Down! Down boy!" But the dog, although hauled away by his handler, continued to bark and bare its teeth. "Whatever's got into you boy?"

Someone in authority ran up to the handler. "Get that dog away from here now!"

"Yes, sarge."

"I'll deal with you later."

"Yes, sarge."

Sue was now bleeding considerably from the wound.

"Get her into the hospital immediately," shouted the doctor. The airmen took off at a run disappearing round the end of a Nissen hut with the doctor following.

"Well, don't just stand there like a load of ninnies! Get him there as well!" barked the sergeant.

"Yes, sir."

Alistair felt himself being carried over the uneven ground and round the same corner Sue had disappeared.

The camouflaged door was still open and Alistair felt himself propelled up a ribbed concrete ramp, which didn't do the pain spreading up from the bottom of his back any good.

Two nurses came running forward. Alistair couldn't believe the huge white headdresses. They wore blue mini capes with white Alice collars over them. An orderly whisked Sue away and he was carried into a side ward and put down on the bed.

A doctor came in.

"Tell me what happened."

"We were in in an explosion – at the old chapel by the railway line –"

"We?"

"Yes, me and Sue."

"Sue? Who's Sue?"

"My friend I came in with – the other stretcher – you must have seen her –"

"No, my friend, you came in here on your own."

*****

Sue lay still with her eyes closed pretending to be unconscious. The bite on her arm itched abominably. She had an almost overwhelming urge to scratch it.

Voices overhead came and went, mostly American. She didn't like what she overheard. Talk of use of sodium pentathol and other injections. They were convinced she was a spy.

She risked raising her eyelids slightly. There was no one about as far as she could see. She opened them fully and looked about her. There was no one in the room. All the other beds were empty. Where was Alistair? Why is she been separated from him? Were they subjecting him to some nameless torture?

She began to feel feverish and a headache clouded her brain. A muscle spasm rippled through her body.

Had she caught something from that wretched dog? A cousin of hers had been out in India. He said rabies was rife out there. If you are bitten you had to have an injection within 24 hours or you were a gonner …

*****

Alistair tried to get up and pain coursed down his legs. He sank back.

"But she's got to be here – she's got to …"

The doctor just stood there looking at him then – "Try and raise your legs."

They felt like lead. He lifted the right leg up a bit. The doctor put his arm underneath his calf. "Press down for me."

Alistair tried. Nothing much happened.

"Now the other one."

Nothing happened. The doctor's mouth twitched. A nurse came in. "Get him to x-ray immediately."

"Yes, doctor."

He was wheeled down the corridor and left outside some double doors covered in danger warnings.

Nothing happened for a long, long time. He strained to sit up but nothing happened.

He drifted off into a doze. Then a voice whispered in his ear.

"Thought we'd got rid of you."

"What?"

A female face focused into view. Not Stephanie.

"We were in an explosion," he whispered. "Where's Sue?"

"Was she with you?"

"Of course she was. But they're denying all knowledge of her."

Not Stephanie looked grave. "I'll make some enquiries. Shan't be long."

He had the x-rays – no padding on the x-ray bed which hurt his lower back no end – and was in the side cubicle by the time she got back.

"The Americans have got her," she said in a subdued voice. "I protested – but she's got no paperwork to prove she's a British citizen. They're still convinced she's a spy – same with you. You know there was an explosion after you escaped last night? They're convinced you had something to do with it. Still, there's not much they can do at the moment – she's unconscious."

"Can I see her?"

"No chance of that I'm afraid. What's wrong with you?"

"It's my back. They haven't said."

"Where were you?"

"In the old Catholic chapel down by the railway crossing. We heard a low droning sound then a scream. Next thing the world exploded."

"Yes. German bombers coming down the coast from a raid on Liverpool. Obviously lost in the fog. Decided to drop their excess bombs to gain height. We'd been tracking them on the radar for some time. We were afraid they were after us. Luckily most of their load dropped in the bog. I'll come by later. For heaven's sake say nothing. Just repeat your name and address and that's all – okay? The Americans are our allies – for now." She left.

Why did she seem to know them now? It was so confusing.

He didn't know how long he lay there as his watch had stopped. Eventually the doctor came back with a clipboard.

"There's not a lot we can do here. This is a minor base military hospital. We're sending you to the hospital in Traethmor – they've got better facilities there."

Away from Sue …

"But …" Then a thought struck him. "What about that dog?"

"What dog?"

"The dog that bit her. That guard dog. Had it had its shots?"

"I'm sure I don't know what you're talking about," the doctor said and swept out.

While he had been lying there a horrible thought occurred to him. Suppose the dog was rabid? It could have been infected with the virus before any symptoms showed.

Without a by-your-leave Alistair was lifted off the bed while still on the stretcher. "What's going on?"

Two American G.Is. looked down on him.

"Doc says you you've got to go to hospital."

"But I'm in one!"

"Not here, dummy, but in a proper one in Traythymoor or something. Can't get the hang of these Welsh names. Okay, Brad, let's get goin'."

"You got it."

He was out in clammy white fog, being hurried towards a military ambulance and loaded into the back, his stretcher being left on the left-hand bed. Someone closed the door and banged on it.

They were off.

Seems they can't get rid of me quick enough. I wonder who's behind all this? Do you think Not Stephanie just wants me away from the Americans? But what about Sue?

The vehicle jolted along the potholed road, the clutch being used awkwardly.

They weren't going long when it ground to a halt with a screech of brakes. He heard raised voices and then footsteps. The doors were flung open and runners pulled out at the back, clattering onto the road surface. Despite the pain he raised himself onto his elbows.

An elderly woman with white stringy hair spread over her pink skull was being wheeled up into the back in a creaking wheelchair, a pink crocheted blanket covering up to her shoulders. She looked in a bad way. A man climbed in behind her, applied the brakes to the chair, and sat down on the unoccupied bed next to her.

He put his hand out and rested it lightly on her shoulder. "Won't be long now Gwen."

"Thank you, doctor." It was barely a whisper.

Alistair looked closely at the man. He could, just could, be a much younger version of the old doctor he and Sue had seen in the surgery when they were being pursued by that bus. But he showed no hint of recognition – why should he? It was 40 or 50 years or so in the future. But we'd met him the camp! It was all too confusing. Upfront the clutch ground in and they were off again.

"Hello, young man – what are you in for?" The doctor asked.

"Seems I did my back in in that explosion."

"The Huns dropping their excess bomb loads into the bog on their way home from a raid on Liverpool I suppose. Won't be the first time."

"How did you get us to stop?"

"Heard you coming. Ran out into the road waving a flag left over from the carnival."

"You could have got run over!"

"Had to take the chance. Gwen's quite poorly."

The old lady moaned.

"There, there, cariad. Be there soon."

A thought struck Alistair. "Have you ever treated a case of rabies?"

"More than once. It's endemic in the bats and foxes."

"Have you any injections?"

"Run out. Why do you ask?"

"I think there might be a case in the camp."

"That's bad. The patient has to have their first injection within 24-hours."

"Is death certain?"

"In most cases, yes."

Alistair froze. "Oh, God."

"Has someone been bitten?"

"Yes."

"Someone you know?"

"Yes."

"When we get to the hospital I'll go to the dispensary and see if they've got any."

"That would be wonderful. Thank you so much."

Alistair felt the ambulance turn left, bounce over a couple of potholes and continue on.

"What's wrong with her?" Alistair whispered.

"Acute appendicitis."

"Couldn't you operate?"

"Shortage of equipment. The base takes it all. They usually have bad burns and fractures through falling objects – though I shouldn't say so."

They lapsed into silence.

Suddenly, there was a loud bang and the doctor was thrown from his seat. The wheelchair slid forwards and slammed into the back of the cab. Alistair clung to the rib attached to the side of the body of the ambulance to prevent being flung to the floor

The doctor picked himself up. "Duw! What in heaven's name was that? Are you all right, cariad?"

The woman moaned softly.

The doctor righted the wheelchair and made his way to the back of the ambulance. He turned back to Alistair. "I'll just have a look outside."

The door creaked open and the doctor disappeared into the fog. The temperature inside dropped abruptly and he shivered.

The doctor reappeared. "We've hit a tree lying across the road. The passenger hit the windscreen and is suffering from shock. The driver hit the wheel and is in considerable pain. Might have cracked a rib or two. We've just gone under a railway arch so I think we are very near Bontfach. I know the farmer there. Perhaps I can persuade him to bring his tractor out and pull the tree out of the way."

"What do I do if your patient gets worse?"

"Nothing much. Talk to her and try and keep her calm. Bontfach's down in a dip beside the river. There's a road running steeply off this road. Hope I won't be long. He slammed the door shut.

'Why on earth is a tree coming down when there's no wind? Hasn't been any for days,' thought Alistair. His thoughts went back to the decommissioned chapel by the railway. *'How could Archie Dugdale be there? He was 40 odd years in the future!* He saw him for what he was now. The genial archaeologist was just a front. He was the high priest of the Greys. Suppose he didn't want Sue to live ... *But how could he know? Had he escaped somehow and brought down the tree? This was all becoming too horrific ...'*

The woman moaned. Alistair heaved himself up onto his elbows. "Doctor won't be long. He's gone to get help."

"It's getting worse, Doctor."

"I said he's gone to get help."

But the woman just moaned.

Far off, but growing louder, he could hear the throaty roar of a tractor coming towards them from the front. *'It must have come across the fields and through a gate onto the road,'* Alistair thought.

There was a jangling of chains, a roar and then a loud cracking and creaking sound as if a large amount of wood was being dragged along the road. The roaring reached fever pitch and the scraping became louder. Then there was more jangling, more dragging. The roaring died away to a steady purring.

The doors were flung open and the doctor appeared holding up the driver who had one arm around the doctor's shoulders. He looked grey in the face. The doctor helped the driver onto the bed on the right across from Alistair.

"I'll have to drive this thing to Traethmor. Hope there aren't any more trees!" He closed the doors.

After a lot of ignition noise and grinding of gears the ambulance lurched forward, gradually picking up speed.

Progress was slow. Driving in fog was never much fun, Alistair thought. Perhaps the headlights were smashed.

There were many twists and turns and grinding of gears during which he felt the ambulance go up and down hills many times until, at last, there was a long descent into Traethmor.

The vehicle turned off to the left and came to a halt. He heard the driver's door open and close and then silence.

The R.A.F. ambulance driver stared gloomily at him.

Then the doors opened and porters in brown overalls looked in. They disappeared and a man in a white coat got into the ambulance, had a look at the woman in the wheelchair and then got the porters to get the runners out to wheel her down. All of this was done in absolute silence which Alistair found unnerving.

A porter came back with an empty wheelchair.

"I'm not sitting up in that!" he said.

"No?"

"I've got a back injury."

"Right. Back in a moment."

Alistair was beginning to think that this was a thoroughly rum do when the village doctor turned up with another doctor who had a stethoscope round his neck and a nurse in full headgear and starched apron.

"Try and raise your right leg. And now your left leg." The doctor's face betrayed no emotion as Alistair lifted his right leg slightly and his left leg not at all. He took out a hammer from his pocket and knocked on each knee. Nothing.

"We'll get you into bed just as soon as one's free. In the meantime we'll put you in a side cubicle. Can you see to it nurse?"

"Yes, doctor."

"How's the old lady?" Alistair asked the village doctor.

"They're going to operate on her as soon as they can. I'll try and drop in on you when I come back to see her. In the meantime I've got to get the ambulance to a garage."

"Is there much wrong with it?"

"I'm no mechanic, but it looks like nothing more than a bent bumper and smashed radiator grille. Good luck!" He strode off.

Two men in brown coats appeared and lifted him on the stretcher off the bed and carefully onto a gurney outside the ambulance.

Mist swirled around the entrance as the doors parted and they pushed him into the fetid heat of the entrance corridor. The smell of antiseptic hung densely in the air.

They turned left and his world view swung dizzily as he looked at the underside of the doorway, was wheeled up between curtained cubicles, pushed into a bay and left.

After all that action he just lay there exhausted for what seemed an age. His mouth was incredibly dry and tasted of cinders. There was no feeling in his legs.

'Oh, God! What am I going to do? Sue's dying by inches miles away, and here I am, unable to move … And I forgot to remind the doctor to get her medication …'

Chapter 27

Alistair's eyes must have closed. A loud commanding voice broke in on him, waking him up.
"Mr Powell?"
He struggled awake.
A thickset woman in a dark blue uniform and starched apron was standing by him. "We'll see if we can make you more comfortable. Nurse will be along in a bit to see you." She swept off.
More waiting.
A nurse materialised by his side with two men who slid him sideways off the stretcher. The pain in the bottom of his back was excruciating and he cried out.
The nurse tried not to show any emotion, but her lips pursed. "Back in a moment."
He could see her speaking to a man in a white coat who nodded and then they both disappeared.
Moments later it seemed they were back.
The man spoke, "Got to get you out of those clothes into a gown so I'm going to give you an injection in your lower back – so if you could roll onto your side for me?"
Alistair struggled onto his side. He felt his trousers being undone and pulled down a bit. There was a sharp pain and then warmth seemed to spread up his body.

"Just lie there for a moment."

The doctor looked at his watch and seemed to be counting. He looked up. "How do you feel?"

"A lot better."

"Good. Right. We'll see if we can get you out of these clothes. You won't be embarrassed, will you? They do this all the time."

Another nurse appeared and drew the curtains round the bed. He supposed he would just have to put up with it.

He was expertly and quickly stripped and inspected for cuts and bruises. They appeared to be satisfied and put him in a hospital gown – one of those awful draughty things with tie tapes up the back.

"We'll get you to X-ray soon."

"But –"

"No buts, Mr Powell!" said one of the nurses smiling sweetly.

"Can anyone tell me what's wrong yet?"

"I'm sorry. That's for the doctor."

There was a lot more waiting. He supposed there always was in hospitals. If only he knew what was happening to Sue. He looked at his watch. It was still stopped. Luckily he could see the ward clock. He adjusted his watch. 7:05. It would be dark outside – would have been for hours. It had been a long day.

He woke up to find himself moving. He looked up. The ceiling beams and strip lights were flicking past and a fetid wind was passing over him.

There was a bump as double doors opened in front of him and he found himself in X-ray.

A man looked up from the clipboard "Mr Powell?"

"Yes," said Alistair wearily. I suppose they have to keep checking.

"Can you sit up?"

He sat up with difficulty. Two men appeared either side and lifted him under the armpits, helping him to a bed with a camera suspended over it from the ceiling.

With a creaking sound of oiled metal sliding over itself the contraption came gliding towards him and then lowered slightly. Someone stood on a stool and pushed a black rectangle into a slot above the lens.

"Lie still for me please," a man in green scrubs said, retiring behind a screen.

There was a whirr and a click.

Then the man in green came out and slid a black rectangle under the bed Alistair was lying on. Again the same procedure.

"Can you tell me anything?"

"That's for the doctor. But my guess is it's no more than a bad bruise."

"Thanks. A bad bruise. Ah, well. Could be worse I s'pose." Alistair was wheeled back to the ward and left again. He fell into a daze.

There was the rattle of a trolley. Something was unceremoniously dumped on the table across the end of his bed. Even from where it was it smelled disgusting. The trolley was about to leave.

"Hey!"

"You want to complain about the meal ?" A loud fat voice from a loud fat woman.

"I would if I could get to it!"

"You can't get up?"

"No."

The woman heaved alongside and pushed the table along the bed up to him and squeaked off.

Up close it was worse. What was it? A slab of brown crust leant drunkenly against brown bits in thick gravy whilst pale green peas cooked to destruction hung about it as if ashamed.

Build me right up that will.

He tried to heave himself up but couldn't.

A man to his right said "You too, eh?"

"Yup."

"Hang on a minute. I'll help you up."

Brown brawny hands gripped him under the armpits and heaved.

"Mr Franks, what are you doing out of bed?" A tall woman in a frilly hat that wouldn't be out of place round a joint of lamb advanced on the man, every inch a scowl.

"Sorry, matron. He couldn't reach 'is dollop."

"All right. Just this once then."

Franks pushed the table towards Alistair and extended a hand. "Albert Franks. Friends call me Albie." Alistair took it gingerly. It was large and sweaty.

"Pleased to meet you Albie."

"So – what you in for then?"

"Bed, Mr Franks," called the matron in an exasperated tone.

Franks winked at Alistair and got back into bed.

"Go on, have a go. It won't eat you!"

"But can I eat it?"

"Gotta keep your strength up."

Alistair tried an exploratory mouthful. It was tepid, chewy and someone had overdone the curry powder. He hated curries – but needs must …"

"So what you in for then?" persisted Albie.

"Did my back in. You?"

"Appendix."

"Didn't you strain your scar just now?"

"Nar. Healing nicely fanks. They say I'll be out soon. Still get these pains though. And they won't give me enough pills to reduce them nor get to sleep. Could do with some of those 'appy pills."

"Happy pills?"

"You know."

Alistair didn't, but thought it best to keep quiet. He grinned instead.

"So what you do then?"

"Journalist."

"Oh, ah. Dug up any juicy cases, then?"

"Not really. It's mostly hard slog trekking round houses interviewing people. What about you?"

Albie grinned. "Ar – You know. Dodgin' and weavin', dodgin' and weavin'."

He's not from round here, Alistair thought. But he might be useful. He wished the beds were closer. He looked round – there didn't seem to be anyone about. He said in a low voice, "I got this friend. She's – you know – in the family way. She wants to know if I can get hold of any pills for it."

"You'll be lucky! Whoever invents them will make a fortune! Just imagine the black market in that!" Albie's eyes gleamed.

Alistair felt the germ of an idea begin to grow in his head. 'Dodging and weaving,' Albie had said. Maybe Albie was what they used to call a 'spiv' or a 'wideboy'. Silly of me anyway – the pill won't be invented for another eight or so years yet and not in the UK until the 1960s. This time slipping was taking a lot of getting used to.

"There must be loads of stuff in the drug cupboard if only I could get my hands on it."

Albie leaned forward "You're talking my language, my son."

"There's no way I can get down there in my condition."

"I've been lyin' 'ere thinkin' I can't do it on my own. But I've said too much already. How do I know I can trust you?"

"It would be too good an opportunity to miss," Alistair said musingly.

"Yeah. Too right." Albie lapsed into silence.

Then they both heard a continuous squeak which sounded like a trolley.

"That's the pill trolley that is," whispered Albie." Coming on its rounds. After that it's lights out."

The rattling came near and two nurses approached with pills and little plastic cups – one doling them out and the other recording what had been given to who on a clipboard.

Alistair found his a bit difficult to swallow with a dry mouth, but he was given a drink of water and the trolley rattled off. He didn't know what they were but the dull pain in his back eased considerably.

Sometime later the lights went out leaving only a low light at the nursing station in the middle of the gangway between the rows of beds up by the doors into the ward. It had files in neat stacks on it with a nurse sitting with her back to the doors so she could look down the length of the ward.

The problem was going to be getting past her.

Alistair was lying awake staring at the ceiling when something white caught his eye coming from the right. It landed on his chest.

It was a paper dart.

He picked it up and squinted at it. The curtain behind his bed was very thin so he could just about read the words 'read this' written on it in block capitals.

He opened it and read, 'The day room to your left has some back stairs that connect all the floors. I'm going to cause a diversion'.

Fine. But what was he supposed to do? And how on earth was he supposed to get past the nurse to the room with the drugs in, wherever it was? Had to be near hadn't it?

Just then someone came in to speak to her. When he looked back Albie had gone.

Not long after, he heard the night nurse pick up the phone. There was a whispered conversation and she got up and left, the swing doors thumping together softly after her.

He looked round for his crutches. The keys might be hanging in the office if they weren't on the nurse's belt.

How had he got himself into this?

Well, the nurse had well and truly gone. He listened for any sound of footsteps. All he could hear was gentle breathing and the occasional snore.

Without crutches it would have been easy to slip through the doors at the end of the ward, but now he was going to have to push hard. They were difficult to budge until he leant his full weight on them.

The door to the office was open. She hadn't had time to lock it. The light level was very low, but he could just make out the rows of keys on the wall next to the window. Light from a street lamp was slanting sideways through a tear in the blackout.

Ah, there it was! Labelled 'Door to drugs cupboard'. He leant a crutch against the wall and lifted it off the hook.

Picking up the crutch he hobbled out of the room and tried the key in the lock on the door next to the office.

It eased open into a room in total darkness. Great! Now what do I do?

He heard footsteps coming and froze. No good standing in the doorway, you idiot! He slipped into the room and was about to close the door when it was thrust inwards.

A torch clicked on, pointing at the floor. "Right, we haven't got long." Albie's voice.

The beam ranged round the shelves.

"Cor! Look at this lot! I should ha' brought a bigger bag!"

Alistair wasn't interested in Albie's plundering – he was hunting in the dim dancing light for anything to do with rabies.

The trouble was that the labels on the bottles and boxes didn't make much sense to him.

Wait a minute! What was that?

"Albie, can I borrow your torch for a minute?"

"Sure. I've almost got what I want. What's your poison?"

"I'm looking for a rabies vaccine."

"Ah, now we get the truth. What you wan' that for?"

"My girlfriend's been bitten by a dog – long story."

"Haven't got time for explanations. What you found?"

"Here. There's something labelled 'RABV'."

"Could be it. Come on, reckon our time's up."

Alistair grabbed a brown box about the size of an A5 sheet of paper and followed Albie out of the room, locking it behind him.

"Where can I put it?" he whispered to Albie.

"Give it 'ere. You leave that to me."

Alistair returned the key to its hook just as he thought he heard the noise of returning footsteps coming up the stairs somewhere.

As quietly as he could he eased himself out through the doors of the office into the corridor and was making for the ward when a low voice said –

"Mr Powell, where are you going?"

"I was – er – just going to the lavatory."

"With your back to me?"

"I – er – forgot something." He turned round to find the night nurse staring at him stonily.

"And what would that be?"

"I needed my wash bag."

The nurse pursed her lips. "You know you shouldn't be out of bed at this hour."

"I'm sorry."

She exhaled slowly and seemed to come to a decision.

"All right, I'll take you."

"Oh. Right. Thanks." At least it would give time for Albie to secrete everything. Thank goodness she didn't notice he didn't have a wash bag.

When he came back the curtains were drawn round Albie's bed. Perhaps he wanted to sort things out without prying eyes.

Feeling tired after his exertions and all the excitement he fell asleep and didn't wake up until the lights came on and the curtains were being drawn.

He looked over to Albie's bed. The curtains were still drawn. A nurse came down the ward and pulled them back. Albie was not there and it seemed plain that the bed had not been slept in. Alistair realised with a sinking heart that he must've gone immediately not only with his purloined drugs but with the precious rabies vaccine as well.

The nurse turned and ran back to the office. He could hear raised voices and then a more senior nurse came out with her and walked sedately down to the unoccupied bed and went through his bedside cupboard, methodically putting the contents on the bed. Slippers, dressing gown, wash bag – nothing else.

They walked back to the office and Alistair could see the more senior nurse pick up the telephone and dial. She was talking rapidly but he couldn't hear anything. Then she appeared to say something like 'What?' She slammed the phone down and came out of the office.

"Nurse!"

Several came running all at the same time.

She tried to stay calm but she had obviously been given some unwelcome news. He could just about hear the word 'wounded' and maybe 'soldiers'.

The nurses immediately spread out and one came to him. "I'm afraid we got to move you. There's a whole lot of wounded coming in and we need the beds. You're ambulatory aren't you?"

"Pardon?"

"Sorry. You can move under your own steam?"
"Yes – I suppose so. But –"
"Get dressed then."
"But –"
She had gone.

It wasn't going to be much fun getting out of this hospital gown and into his clothes. He got out of bed with difficulty and bent down even though it hurt, opening the door to his cupboard. He pulled his clothes out and something fell out onto the floor with a thump – the brown box – so Albie hadn't nicked it after all!

But how to get it out of the hospital? Bundle it up in your hospital gown and hold it under one arm. What, with crutches? He needed a stick – and fast.

He looked around. Nothing. Wait a minute – there was one up in the corner at the other end of the ward. He made towards it painfully. The nurses were too busy to pay much heed.

Coming back with his prize he got out of his horrible draughty hospital gown and pulled on his clothes sitting on the bed. Bundling up the box inside the gown he started for the ward doors.

"Where are you going?" a female voice demanded

He turned, wearily.

"We've got all the other patients in the day room ready to be moved. You'd better join them."

He started off down the ward. Albie had said there were stairs off the day room connecting it with all the other floors. Perhaps he could …

The day room was crowded. Not a seat to be had. Several woebegone patients were even standing, one with a drip in his arm attached to a movable stand. It was pandemonium. Nobody was in charge.

He went through the doors onto the landing and looked down the stairs. It was a very long way down. Those high Victorian ceilings.

But if that was the only way down out of here then that had to be it. But how was he going to manage the descent with a stick and the parcel and hang onto the handrail? The only way was to make a sort of rucksack out of the gown and hang it round his neck over his back. This proved difficult, but eventually he did it, keeping out of the way of the window in the door.

He began the descent.

About halfway down the muscles in his legs began to tremble. He must keep going. Keep going. Think of her face.

After an age he reached the bottom.

There must be a lift somewhere. There had to be. There was a corridor off to his left so he took it. It led through a series of storerooms which ended in a lift. Thank heavens! He went in, pulled the grille across with difficulty, pulled the inner grille across and pressed the button marked 'O'.

The lift clanked and, with agonising slowness, began to descend.

When it finally settled with a bump and he had wrestled the two grilles open he found himself in a cold, damp, concreted area. There was a huge concertina door and beside it another door with a window in it. Through this he could see a road and some trees.

He tried the door. Locked.

Maybe you can get the concertina door open?

There was a red knob. He pressed it.

With a grinding, creaking sound it began to move. It was making a heckuva racket. Suppose someone was watching? Did they have CCTV cameras in those days? He didn't know.

Now it was open just enough to squeeze through. He stopped pressing and the grinding halted.

He was out. But where to now? How to get back to Sue with no money?

He stood in the road and listened. Not a sound. He began walking.

The road led to an avenue of trees that fed into the town centre. Hardly anybody about. And no cars. Must be the petrol rationing.

The hospital had been at the bottom of the hill so – look for a hill. And there it was – rearing up to his right. It looked one hell of a climb, especially with his back.

The longest journey starts with the first step – and all that.

He got about halfway up and sat down on a convenient bench exhausted. He was never going to make it. It was too far. He was so tired. No traffic had passed him. He looked towards the rising ground and trees opposite and groaned.

He was never going to make it.

Chapter 28

The noise of a grating gearchange made him jump.
A dark green Land Rover was labouring up the hill.
Now or never.
He levered himself up and stood in the road, thumb extended. He'd heard it worked in those days.
The vehicle obligingly ground to a halt.
"Need a lift?" A man in a flat cap leaned out of the window.
"I certainly do."
"Hop in then."
He opened the creaking passenger door and heaved himself onto a cracked leather seat.
Too late he saw the camouflaged uniform. "Where to then?"
"Ah. My mistake."
"What's the matter with you? Do you want a lift or not?"
He had to get to her. He felt his mouth opening and closing like a frog.
"Haven't got all day you know."
"Er – yeah."
"Right, then." The man put the car grittily into gear. It slid backwards a bit.
"Come on old girl," Alistair heard the man mutter under his breath.

The engine roared and gripped. The man heaved a sigh. "That's it, old girl."

They ground up the hill.

"So, where to then?"

Alistair took a deep breath – too near and yet – too far away and … "Aberceldy."

"Any particular bit?"

In for a penny … "The rocket range."

They were at the top of the hill now. The man behind the wheel stood on the brakes and looked round at him. "WHAT?"

Alistair went on the offensive, "Come on, it's no secret. Everybody in the village knows about it." The man put the handbrake on and sat staring at him while the engine idled in the background.

"And why do you want to go there?"

"My girlfriend's there. In the base hospital. She's suffering from rabies and I'm taking the vaccine to her – look."

He pulled the brown cardboard box out of the hospital gown.

The man took it and examined it. "And when was this?"

"I think it was a couple of days ago."

"You think?"

"I've been in hospital. Road accident. Long story."

The man looked at him for a long time, pursed his lips and then took the handbrake off. "Then we'd better get there sharpish!" And he put his foot down.

It was frightening, bouncing along the potholed roads as the man wrenched the Rover round tight bends and up and down hills. They didn't seem to be any straight roads much. With no seat belts he found himself gripping the door handle or bracing himself against the dashboard.

Soon they were thundering down Aberceldy High Street and Alistair was forced to confront the situation.

He didn't have a plan once they got there.

Borderlands

The man reached under his seat holding the juddering wheel with one hand and swapped over his flat cap for a hat with a badge on it.

They drove up to the gates. Nobody was about. The man swore under his breath and leaned heavily on the horn.

A soldier came darting out of the guard hut behind the barrier, doing up his jacket, came round to the driver's door and saluted.

"Don't just stand there man, get it up!"

"Yes, sir, Captain, Sir!"

"And where's your cap?"

"In the 'ut sir."

"Well it should be on your head! Now get a move on!"

The squaddie raised the barrier and stood saluting awkwardly.

"Can't be away five minutes – place goes to rack and ruin," the man said loudly to the windscreen.

The Land Rover juddered to a halt outside what Alistair took to be some kind of command post.

"Well, jump to it, man! No time to lose! Oh, I see you can't. Need a hand?"

"No, I can get out all right – I think."

"Come on then."

With Alistair in the rear, hobbling along on his stick, they entered the building where a non-com officer was sitting in a bare room behind a table checking files.

"What did you say her name was?" The captain asked, turning to Alistair.

"Sue Masters."

The other man looked up. "A civilian, sir? Not many of them here – apart from the boffins."

"Well, look her up."

The man turned to a file and flicked through it. "Nobody here of that name, sir."

"Do the Americans have her?" Alistair asked

"Wouldn't know that, sir. I only got records for the British."

The captain turned smartly on his heels and looked sideways at Alistair. "Come with me."

They came out of the building, turned left and right along a concrete path to a large hut whose entrance was flanked by two Americans with 'MP' in white on their dark green steel helmets.

"We're looking for your commanding officer."

"And you are, Sir?" the one on the right asked.

"Captain Marshall."

"He's off base."

"Well, we'll see his second in command then."

"Can't do that sir. He's busy."

"Is he now?" Well, tell him this man," indicating Alistair, "has drugs vital for the war effort. See if that makes him less busy."

The MP chewed for a moment, spat out his chewing gum on the concrete at the captain's feet and turned sharply, entering the dark of the door. He seemed to be gone a long time.

Abruptly a middle-aged, rather portly man appeared, his collar undone, his hat askew and buttons straining over his belly. He was chewing or sucking at something the stick of which stuck out from the side of his mouth.

The captain saluted smartly and the American, who appeared to be a major, saluted lazily and leant sideways, propping himself up on the door frame.

"What can I do for you captain – er?"

"Marshall, sir."

"Well, what can I do for you Captain Marshall?" he said lazily.

"We have reason to believe that you are holding a British civilian, Sue Masters."

"And what if we are?"

"We have a drug here that is urgently needed to be administered."

"What sort of drug?"

"Anti rabies."

The major levered himself off the frame and stood up straight "Rabies?"

"That's what I said, sir."

"And this occurred here, on this base?"

"So I believe, sir."

"Are you aware, captain, that this Masters is a Heini spy?"

"Do you have evidence – sir?"

"My friend is dying while we stand here arguing!" Alistair blurted out.

"And who might you be, Buster?"

"I'm –"

"You're the other spy aren't you? Put you two Limeys together and who knows what would happen. Tell you what – you give me the drug and we'll administer it."

"Oh no. I need to see her."

"I think you know the protocol in these matters," Captain Marshall said.

The major scowled. His commanding officer was a stickler for protocol and he didn't want to be carpeted on his return. He turned his back and gestured for them to come in.

But the moment Alistair crossed the threshold the MPs closed ranks, barring the captain from entering. Alistair found himself alone in a dim corridor behind the retreating form of the major who turned left at the end of the corridor. Alistair followed and found him standing beside an open doorway. Within was a bed with two female nurses in white jackets and skirts – one with her back to the door. She turned and Alistair could see Sue, pale and drenched in sweat, convulsively turning her head from side to side.

Alistair rushed forward, pushing past the major, and put the precious box on the bed. Looking down at her he grasped one of her hands, holding it tight to his chest.

"It's me, Alistair, I'm here. You're going to be all right."

But Sue just twitched, turning her head from side to side, oblivious.

"How long has she been like this?" he demanded of the nurses.

"Since 9.15 this morning."

"I have the vaccine here in this box."

"It may be already too late, sir," said one of the nurses.

"You've got to try!"

She picked the box off the bed and tore off the seal. Inside the box were cardboard compartments and in them were a number of small bottles with rubber discs in their lids and, alongside, a syringe with a packet of needles. The other nurse was already putting on a pair of surgical gloves and picking up the syringe. She plunged a needle into a rubber disc and drew out a sample of liquid, flicking the syringe with a finger and squirting it experimentally into a nearby sink. The other nurse swabbed Sue's arm with alcohol.

Sue continued to thrash, but the other nurse managed to hold her still with difficulty. The needle was inserted into her upper arm.

"What happens now?"

"You can let go of her hand now, sir."

"But what happens now?"

The nurse with the syringe looked at him sternly. "Now we wait."

"How long?"

"Who can say?"

Alistair sensed someone standing behind him. He turned round to see the major.

"In my office please."

He turned on his heel and strode off.

Alistair hesitated, but then the man turned and glared at him. Well, there was nothing more he could do here. He followed.

There were so many twists and turns that he became disorientated. It must be a big building. Eventually the American reached a half glazed door of frosted glass with 'Major A.R.

Krabowitz' on a nameplate screwed onto the wood below the glass. He thrust open the door and went in. Alistair followed to find another occupant of the room sitting behind a bare trestle table at right angles to the major's desk. Stephanie. Or rather Not Stephanie.

Krabowitz sat down at a heavy oak desk strewn with papers and a tier of 'In' and 'Out' trays on the end nearest to Alistair. A wooden chair faced it.

"Captain Chambers has some questions for you."

So it was her! Why was she pretending it wasn't?

Stephanie looked keenly at Alistair. "So you escaped – but you came back. Why was that?"

"Surely you know? Sue was bitten by a guard dog after we were captured. There was no vaccine on the base so I went to get some. And now I've come back and delivered it."

Stephanie turned to the major. "I have questioned this man intensely already. His story, although it has some unusual elements – some *very* unusual elements – has the ring of truth. In my opinion he is deluded, even living in a fantasy world – but he is *not* a spy. He would not, in my opinion, have voluntarily come back here but would have made himself scarce and reported back to his masters. I have spoken to Captain Marshall, who found him sitting on a bench halfway up the hill out of Traethmor begging for a lift back here."

The major leant back in his chair and pursed his lips. Alistair noticed he was no longer sucking a lollipop or whatever he had been before. He had lost the look of slight amusement and was deadly serious. He looked up at the ceiling and then down straight across at Alistair.

"I have every faith in the captain's judgement. We have, you may say, er – *an understanding*." He smiled briefly in Stephanie's direction. "You are free to go – but if anyone catches you – *anyone at all* – in this camp again, you will be arrested and shot as a spy under wartime regulations." He leaned forward and stared at Alistair. "Do I make myself entirely clear?"

"But ..."

"I release you into the custody of the captain here. See" – he looked pointedly at Stephanie – "he doesn't enter this sector again. I hold you personally responsible."

Stephanie stood up and saluted, "Yes, sir."

"Run along then." The major looked down at his paperwork and sighed.

Outside in the corridor she turned to him angrily and hissed, "Why on earth did you come back? I let you go."

"You don't get it, do you? I love her."

Stephanie looked up and down the corridor. She held out her hands imploringly, "But you're meant for something far greater."

"What do you mean?"

"Why do you think they're drawn to you?"

Alistair passed a hand over his throbbing brow. "You're not making any sense."

"Come into my office and I'll brew some tea."

"And that's supposed to make me feel better is it?"

She stared at him. "Oh do stop being so difficult and come on!"

She strode off and Alistair trailed after her, thoroughly confused.

After several confusing twists and turns she opened a door into a comfortable looking office. There was a desk and a chair, yes, but also leather armchairs and a sofa. He sat down in an armchair and she went over by the window and set about boiling a kettle, spooning loose tea from a tin into a brown pot on the sink drainer in the corner. An electric water heater was poised over it, screwed to the wall.

"Sugar?"

"No, thanks."

When the tea was brewed she sat down opposite him in the other armchair.

He took an exploratory sip out of the green china cup.

"So you really are Stephanie?"

"That's one of the names they call me."

Alistair ignored this. It was getting too complicated already.

"So why pretend not to be?"

Stephanie spread her hands and then dropped them into her lap in an exasperated gesture "It's complicated."

"So, how come you know stuff that hasn't happened yet?"

"Because we can travel in time."

"We? Who's we?"

"Archie and me and the doctor."

"But Archie's just – evil!"

"Yerss. You see he and I have chosen different paths." She paused and drank her tea. "He's here to exploit the situation and I'm here to stop him somehow, but you have to lead them to safety first."

"Who?"

"The people in the Bardo."

"What's the Bardo?"

"Okay – you would call them the people under the stairs. They are the dead from different eras – airmen and women who died before their time. What you didn't see were the people standing behind them – all those unfortunates who met untimely deaths in air disasters – Manchester United football club, Daghammaskjold, Samara Machelle, John Garang, Amelia Earhart possibly – I haven't made my mind up about her. She has a lot of unresolved ... issues. They want to move on. To go home."

Alistair felt a stab of memory – that football imprint on the window in the kitchen at his house – they had been trying to attract his attention all along.

"But why air disasters? Why airmen and women?"

"Jones was an airman – the previous owner of your house. He took off on a flight and never came back. They're drawn to his house and his memory."

Alistair could see that she seemed more and more lost in her own thoughts. "Amelia tried to kill Archie by attracting the German bombers, but he just walked free of the wreckage by side slipping in time just as I knew he would."

"But that would mean leaving the base, leaving Sue – I can't do it."

Stephanie's attention snapped back to him, "But you have to look at the bigger picture – she is superfluous."

Alistair was on his feet before he knew it, leaning over her. "Superfluous?" He felt like hitting her. "How can – how can – one person be superfluous? Everyone is important in their own way. No, I won't do it. Not unless she comes with us."

"But she's very sick. She might die on even that short journey."

Alistair sat down again. Then a spark flickered into life in his mind. If he could just take her back to 1990 where they had better drugs, better care … then … But by just by entering that cupboard under the stairs could he be sure that they would go back to 1990? They could end up anywhere in time – couldn't they? The situation could become much much worse …

He held out his hands imploringly. "We have to take that chance. I won't leave her behind."

Stephanie looked up at the ceiling, shook her head and looked at him.

"All right." She sighed heavily. "I was never going to get you to fall in love with me. Not this time. But you did love me – once."

What? he thought – but didn't dare say it.

"So what do we do?"

Stephanie got up and looked at the floor. "I have to convince the major to let her go. He may be glad to get rid of her – off his hands while his boss's away. Maybe he'll see the merit in her getting better care in a proper hospital. She paused and looked angrily at Alistair. "You know he was going to detain you as a spy and have you shot. I managed to talk him out of it. *Just you remember that.*"

She strode out of the room, pulling the door open savagely. Then she came back in, "Well, don't just sit there! Come on!"

They made their way back to the major's office. Arriving there Stephanie rapped smartly on the door.

"Come!

She looked round at Alistair, put a finger to her lips, motioned him away from the door and went in. Minutes later, during which he heard raised angry voices, the major came storming out of his office and without giving Alistair a second glance went up the corridor. Alistair had to walk fast to keep up with him and Stephanie. His back paining him, he struggled to follow her round the twists and turns.

Sue was lying quite still with her eyes closed. Alistair looked at one of the nurses who shook her head slowly.

Krabowitz turned and looked at Stephanie. "Just get her out of here."

Obviously, thought Alistair, he doesn't want any dead spies on his conscience.

The nurses got the silent body onto a trolley and wheeled it along the corridors and out into the late afternoon watery sunshine.

A truck with a red cross on a white circle on its green tarpaulin was already drawn up outside his engine idling.

The inside of the back the truck was very bare – hardly any medical facilities at all. There was drip stand bolted to the floor, a cupboard with a lock on it and two bare mattresses with rather grubby white sheets on them either side. Purely functional for getting the wounded away from the battlefront he supposed.

The nurses pushed the trolley up a removeable wooden ramp and lifted Sue onto one of the beds. Alistair sat on the other one and held her hand. It was cold and clammy. Holding it tightly against his chest he wished with every fibre that he could will some life and warmth into it. The canvas flaps at the back were pulled roughly closed leaving him in semi darkness.

Where was Stephanie? He assumed she was up front with the driver – suppose she hadn't left the base? No – surely she must be there?

With a jolt the truck moved off, executed a three-point turn and then they were off, rumbling over the ridged bumpy concrete of the base, pausing briefly, he assumed, at the main gate and then out onto the road where the rumbling gave way to the smoother hum of the tarmac.

There was a pause, he thought, at the junction of the road to the base and the curve of the road where it crossed the river over a bridge and then the truck accelerated away down the long straight road into the village.

Save for the noise of the engine all was eerily quiet – almost as if they were suspended in time.

Cold fear clutched at his heart. The time difference must be sweeping up the village – if there was any village anymore? There must be – otherwise the driver would have stopped in wonderment. But then who was driving this thing? If it was Stephanie she would be unfazed by any changes. Suppose the house was no longer there? He gripped Sue's hand even tighter "Hang on, my love," he whispered.

Suddenly there was a shout and a blast of light so brilliant that the ribs of the truck over which the canvas was stretched stood out brilliantly and the canvas seemed to disappear momentarily. The truck lurched to the left, almost throwing them to the floor, engine roaring, and then turned, seemingly on two wheels, as if going round some obstacle, righted itself and accelerated down the road. There was another flash, of lesser power this time, and then the gunning of another engine behind them that receded into the distance.

The truck veered to the right and then stopped abruptly, throwing him sprawling on the bed.

A wild eyed Stephanie, her hair plastered to her face which was red and seemed to have scorch marks on it, appeared tearing back the canvas.

"Pick her up and give her to me. Come on! *Run!*"

Alistair handed the unmoving Sue down to Stephanie standing in the road outside the house. He jumped down off the back of the truck. Bloody hell! That hurt!

He looked up the road towards the sound of an engine screaming towards them.

A flash of light and the smell of singed wood came from behind him. A hole had appeared where a window to his house had been. Stephanie was already climbing through it, holding Sue

"Come on!" she shouted.

He clambered through the still smouldering charred remains and into the sitting room. She handed Sue to him.

"I'll hold him off. You know what to do."

"But –"

"Go!"

He stumbled into the hall, turned right and went through the open door into the cloakroom in almost total darkness, then through the door to the right and into mist which had sprung up instantly.

Far off he could see a dim light and again entered the circle on the floor. The mist dissipated.

There were whispers all round him.

"Ah, good, you've brought her," said the voice of Amelia Earhart behind him.

He turned slowly and she was there. "You are the Lamplighter but she is The Key."

Sue's eyes flickered open. "I've had such a strange dream," she said, "Where are we?"

"In the world under the stairs," he said.

"Oh."

"How do you feel?"

"Like I've been lying in a long dark tunnel."

"Indeed you have, my dear," said a man close by. He looked vaguely familiar from press photographs, Alistair thought, but he couldn't place him.

The man spoke gently, "Just stretch out your hand my dear, now your arm."

A point of light grew at the end of her index finger and as she moved it upwards and downwards in the dark outside the cone of light a slit appeared through which pearly light shone. As the slit broadened into a gap, fuzzy outlines of buildings appeared – domes, spires and columns reaching into the sky.

Whispering voices streamed past them until all was silent.

A voice spoke from behind him. It was Amelia again.

"Goodbye, Lamplighter. Perhaps we will meet again."

Soundlessly the gap snapped shut leaving them alone in the dark.

Alistair shivered. All pervasive cold was invading his body. The mist was back again.

The ground moved underneath him and pebbles chinked. He staggered, desperate to keep his footing. The mist became chilling fog, shifting as he looked about him.

The house walls had gone.

Alistair shivered and looked down at Sue. Her eyes were closed tight and she looked paler than ever.

The story continues in Borderlands 2:
The Colour of Shadows.

The author wishes to thank, in no particular order,
the following for their help,
patience and endless encouragement.

Alison Reed

Anne Nicholls

Nick Daws

The Walsall Writers Circle

Borth Writers

The Janus Effect

"Nice crisp prose, emotional intelligence and a storyline that kept me reading."
(Ian Watson, SF author)

"Fast paced SF with echoes of *The Matrix* and *Doctor Who* ... Very interesting speculations about the nature of time travel ... Intelligent SF ... A good read."
(Nick Dawes, journalist and author)

*****

The Xandra Function

"Intrigue and romance suffuse this SF thriller with warmth and charm. It brings the age-old tales of the relationship between artists and their creations up-to-date as game avatars collide with their human gods"
(Justina Robson, author)